D0861261

DEAD JACK:
BOOK 1

Also by James Aquilone

Madness & Mayhem

Websites

DeadJack.com

HomunculusHouse.com

Facebook.com/OfficialDeadJack

JamesAquilone.com

JAMES AQUILONE

Enjoy!

— James Aquilone

12.1.16

HOMUNCULUS
HOUSE

Published by Homunculus House
Staten Island, New York

Copyright © 2016 by James Aquilone

All rights reserved. No part of this book may be reproduced or transmitted in any form or by any means without written permission of the publisher.

This book is a work of fiction. Names, characters, businesses, places, events, and incidents are either the products of the author's imagination or used in a fictitious manner. Any resemblance to actual persons, living or dead, or actual events is purely coincidental.

Portions of "The Kraken" by Alfred Lord Tennyson are used in chapters 3 and 4.

Cover, map, and interior art by Ed Watson
Edited by Tim Marquitz
Proofread by Eve Conte Seligman

ISBN-10: 1-946346-00-4
ISBN-13: 978-1-946346-00-1

For Jenn,
who's more addictive than fairy dust

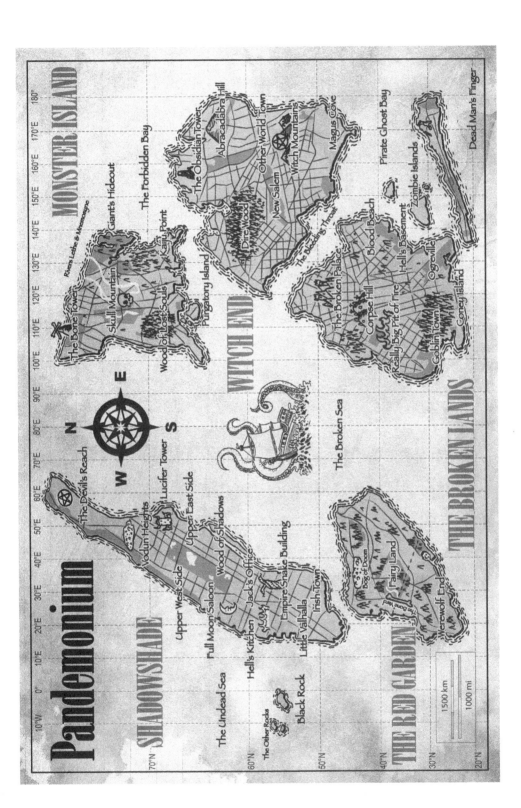

CONTENTS

Dead Jack and the Pandemonium Device

1. Waiting for My Wee-Man   1
2. The Green and the Furious   9
3. Ship of Fools   17
4. Kraken Bait   33
5. Down and Out in the Broken Lands   45
6. The Best-Laid Plan   53
7. And Into the Fire   59
8. Like a Bat Out of Hell   69
9. I Found My Thrill on Corpse Hill   75
10. They Built This City on Rock and Bones   85
11. Dinner for Demons (and Assorted Other Monsters)   97
12. A Room Without a View   105
13. Beneath the Palace of the Arseholes   113
14. A Zombie by Any Other Name   123
15. Return of the White Blob   129
16. A Stroll Down Mnemosyne Lane   133
17. A God Reborn   143
18. Flying the Fiendish Skies   149
19. Monster Island Mash   155
20. Interdimensional Baby Got Back   161
21. The Pandemonium Device Is Fully Operational   167
22. Fear and Loathing in ShadowShade   187

The Case of the Amorous Ogre   193
Bonus Material: Incident on Black Rock   213
Acknowledgments   221
About the Author   225

WAITING FOR MY WEE-MAN

I reached into my jacket for a Lucky Dragon once the shakes began. The undead aren't known for their dexterity so I had a bit of fun getting that hellfire stick. I was like a drunken mummy trying to do jazz hands. I burned off half the skin on my left index finger lighting the damn thing. That made three fingers now that were practically nothing but bone. If this continued, I'd end up a skeleton inside a cheap suit and fedora. I doubted anyone would notice.

Being a member of the great unwashed dead isn't all bad, though. I was happy for my dulled sense of smell. The alleyway stunk like rotten cabbage and sour apples.

I had tried everyone in downtown ShadowShade, but no one was holding. Out of desperation, I came here to Irish Town in search of Fine Flanagan, my old dealer.

Without dust, the hunger becomes overpowering, and when I'm hungry, no one's safe. I'd eat my own dead granny.

I had been waiting in the alley behind Finn McCool's Pub for at least an hour before the leprechaun appeared.

Flanagan isn't your typical lep. First off, he's not that short. Maybe five-foot-two in his pointy shoes. He's broad-shouldered, barrel-chested, and someone you don't want to mess with. He also has the saltiest mouth in all the Five Cities of Pandemonium.

As he entered the alley, he sang:

"There once was a fellow McSweeney who spilled some gin on his weenie..."

With a large sack slung over his shoulder, he swaggered past the reeking dumpsters full of what must have been hundred-year-old cabbage.

"Just to be couth, he added vermouth. Then slipped his girl-friend a martini..."

"Sorry to interrupt that charming little ditty," I said, slipping out of the shadows as I blew smoke out of all the holes in my face. All nine. Real bad-ass.

The lep stopped deader than my libido. Like I'd caught him bathing naked in his pot of gold. (Leprechauns don't really have pots of gold, by the way, but they are known to carry sweet, sweet fairy dust, the closest thing to heaven in this godforsaken world. And Fine Flanagan had the finest.)

The sack jerked and the lep gripped it tighter.

"What's in the bag, Flanny? Someone didn't pay their vig?" I noticed the lep's fashion sense had changed since I last saw him. He wore a green duster that hung to the ground, but there was no pointy hat on his head. His curly red hair blew in the wind. Leps love hats almost as much as their shoes. And his shoes, I noticed, weren't even pointy. They were square-toed boots. What the holy heck?

"None of your fookin business," the lep said. "Now, if you wouldn't be minding, I have better tings to do than conversate with a zombie. I be needing to get to me apartment." When the lep took a step forward, I blocked his way.

"Look, meat bag, I don't be wanting any trouble tonight," he said.

"No trouble. I'm just looking for dust."

The lep exploded into laughter. He actually placed his hand over his belly. A real guffaw.

"You fookin dust head. Oh, Jackie boy, I thought maybe you was on a case. I should have known what you was after. All you zombies are the same. You people are the dumbest pieces of filth in Pandemonium. Just soulless, corpse-faced, brain-licking ghouls."

I told you he had a mouth on him. "Nope. Never licked a brain. Total myth."

"Mouth-breathing, empty-husk, meat-headed, motherless bags of bones, the whole lot of you."

"Keep going."

"You're wasting me precious time."

"Just a gram, Flanny. The hunger is starting to eat through my innards."

"You have innards? Figured it's all just sludge inside you by now. Like ya fookin brain."

"The last time I went cold turkey, it ended real bad for some fairies. I went wilder on them than a pack of weres. I'm still not welcome in the Red Garden."

"You ain't threatening now, are you, ya dead dick?" He smiled, exposing the four or five teeth left in his mouth. I heard he was quite the boxer back in his day.

My hands shook and my bones rattled as I held them up. Flanny probably thought I was trying to conjure a demon. I dropped the hellfire stick and ground it out with my shoe. "I'm desperate."

"Then you're out of luck. I don't deal anymore. I have new opportunities."

There was a *clink*, like a glass bell, from inside the sack and then it shot up in the air. Flanagan nearly lost his grip but managed to pull the canvas bag back down. The lep shot me a look so dirty I thought of taking my first bath in seventy years.

"What's in the sack, Flanny? A sentient beer keg?"

"None of ya fookin business, you filthy corpse."

"Does Dana know what you're up to?"

"Don't you be talking about that blessed woman. This is none of ya business."

"What if I told your leprechaun queen you were up to some unsavory stuff? She might just kick you out of the club. Unaffiliated leprechauns aren't treated very well in Pandemonium, are they?"

The lep spit out a laugh like it was venom. "I don't have to be worrying about that, zombie. You are the one who needs to worry. This is going to be your last night in Pandemonium." The fairy swung the sack into my crotch. I flew into the wall, and

Flanagan took off down the alley. Fortunately, I have a dulled sense of pain so I easily shook off the between-the-legs shot. (As for my zombie genital situation, the less said about that the better.) Still, something in me snapped. Maybe my hunger had reached its apex, or maybe I didn't like the way he called me a filthy corpse. Either way, I pounced on him like a lycan on a moonpie. I don't even remember feasting on the little guy, I was in such a blood frenzy. I do remember him tasting damn delicious, though, like smoked sausage and sweet beer. Then Oswald, Pandemonium's most obnoxious creature and my associate, appeared out of nowhere.

I sat on the ground, gnawing on a leg bone, when the alley filled with a blinding light. I continued eating. Like I said, it was damn good, and I hadn't eaten in so long. The light died out and I saw the Studebaker—my Studebaker. The driver's-side door opened and out slid the homunculus.

The little bugger stared at me, not saying a word, his X-shaped eyes unblinking. This was supposed to shame me. But I'm a revenant (which is a fancy way of saying zombie). I'm beyond shame.

I took a bite out of Flanagan's calf. It was stringy, but I wasn't complaining.

"I cannot express how very disappointed I am in you." Oswald tried to sound tough, but when you're all of eight inches and nothing but a marshmallow with a mouth, the effect is underwhelming. No one knows what Oswald is, or was. The best description I've come up with is a homunculus, which is another way for me to say I have no idea. I think I'd rather not know where he came from. It would most likely lead to trouble and Oswald is plenty of trouble already.

The sack rolled down the alley.

"What's that?" Oswald said.

I licked the lep's shin. Salty with just a hint of sweetness. It just made me hungrier.

"Hey, dummy!" Oswald shouted. "Let me remind you that you're eating a leprechaun in the middle of Irish Town!"

I sprang up—as best a zombie can spring up, which meant I awkwardly repositioned my bones into a standing position. I stepped over to the sack and picked it up. I opened the bag, but wasn't prepared to find what I did.

Mr. Obvious said, "Is that a naked baby inside a glass jar?"

"I'm sorry for ever calling you a terrible detective, Oswald. You figured it out on the very first try."

The dope smiled.

I stood the glass jar up. The baby looked at us with curious silver eyes.

"Maybe this is like those ships you find in bottles," I said.

"How did you get in there, little guy?" Oswald asked.

The fact that he didn't cry should have alarmed me, but I was still on a high from my leprechaun buffet. I wasn't thinking straight.

The baby pointed at the top of the jar. He was a cute little fellow. Pink and soft and full of rolls. A mass of golden curls covered the top of his head.

The observant marshmallow said, "I think he wants you to remove the glass stopper and let him out."

The fact that the baby didn't pop off the glass stopper himself should have made me wonder, but Oswald distracted me with his prattling.

I removed the stopper.

The hole certainly didn't seem big enough for a baby to fit through, even a naked one, but that didn't stop him.

He slid out of the bottle like he was a piece of taffy. But instead of falling onto the ground as a normal baby would, he floated into the air. The large, black wings that had unfurled from his back helped a lot with that, I think. The now-winged baby stopped just out of our reach, shot me a dirty look, gave me the finger, and disappeared into the blood-red sky of Pandemonium, going north. Bye-bye, evil baby.

I wasn't able to conjure up one of my famous ripostes, though, because at that moment two irate leprechauns barreled towards us.

2

THE GREEN
AND THE FURIOUS

"I'm driving!" I shouted as I ran for the car (though it was more like power-shambling).

The leps made a beeline for us. They must have come out of Finn McCool's. One was dressed in a red overcoat and pants. A pointy hat bobbed on his head. At least there was no bell on it. He was most likely a clurichaun, a meaner, nastier, more inebriated leprechaun. He looked like a sauced Saint Nick. The other was dressed in traditional green, a real stereotypical lep, right down to the buckles on his shoes. He was probably born with a four-leaf clover in his mouth.

We made it into the car just as the Irish fairies reached us.

"You bastard, you et Flanagan!" the clurichaun screamed. So much for getting away with eating a leprechaun in Irish Town.

"Where's the fookin IDB?" the other shouted.

I had no idea what he was talking about, but I didn't have time to rack my brain because I sat in amazement as Little Red picked up what was left of Flanagan's arm and banged it against the passenger window. Meanwhile, his comrade stood on the hood kicking at the windshield with his pointy shoes. Good luck causing damage with those leprechaun loafers. Maybe he'd tickle the windshield to death.

"What's an IDB?" Oswald asked.

I threw the Studebaker in reverse, gunned the engine, and we flew backwards. The clurichaun gave out a banshee-like screech. I think I ran over his foot. Oh well. He could always cobble himself a new pair of clown shoes. The other lep fell backwards and slid halfway off the hood, but somehow managed to grab hold of the grille.

The car took a hard bounce as it hit the street. I swerved and jammed on the brake, hoping that would knock the lep off the Studebaker. No chance. This lep was a regular Harold Lloyd. He flipped back on the hood and glared at me.

I threw the car in drive and shot forward. Now with two hood ornaments.

Like some creature emerging from the primordial soup of existence, the lep crawled up the hood and grabbed onto the windshield wipers. Now that he was up close I could see he had a rat face. Pointy nose, eyes too close together, sharp, little teeth jutting over his lip.

"You fookin brain-licker!" rat face shouted.

"What's with the brain-licker business with you guys?" I said.

"Do you know something about me I don't?"

"When I get me hands on you, you're gonna wish for death." The lep was seething, practically foaming at the mouth. His bloodshot eyes bore into me.

"Take Bleak Street," Oswald said. "It's a mess with potholes. Maybe it'll knock him off."

I turned east and blasted onto Bleak Street like a hawkman raiding a basilisk nursery. We immediately nose-dived into a crater-sized pothole. The Studebaker bucked like a wild kraken, but the lep had a grip of iron.

"I'm going to start with ya head, ghoul," the little guy said, his red beard glistening with spittle.

"You make a nice hood ornament," I said. "A little mouthy, though."

"You fookin bastard! I'm going to stick ya head up ya decayed arse."

With a finger, the leprechaun etched strange symbols on the dusty windshield. I admit I hadn't washed the Studebaker in forever and, by that, I literally mean forever. It had never felt the soft touch of a chamois. It was a miracle I could even see through the windshield. The lep squiggled a row of sigils, no doubt working some magic to seize the engine or turn me into a toad or put a pointy hat on my head. I destroyed his nefarious plans with a simple turn of a switch. I laughed as the windshield wipers swept the fairy's symbols away. The lep's face grew redder than the clurichaun's jacket. He ripped off the wipers, and then used them to whack at the windshield.

The Studebaker bounced like an excited goblin as I managed

to hit every pothole on the street. The lep stopped smashing the windshield and now held on for dear life. Then I spotted the mother of all potholes. It was a ditch, really. I hit the gas and we sailed into the hole, hard. I immediately lost control. We slid toward the sidewalk. The lep's body swung out to the side as he held on to the hood with one hand. One of his pointy shoes flew off.

A group of posh vampires drinking blood toddies at an outdoor café panicked, instantly turned into bats, and flew off. My front tire jumped the curb and turned over a chair or three, but I managed to steer the car back onto the road. I floored it, going farther downtown, when an orc biker came zooming down Bleak Street and tore off my passenger-side mirror. As the demon flew by, he screeched something about me being a no-good, soulless husk. I thought about chasing him down and getting his insurance info, but I had other fish to fry.

A car behind us honked like crazy.

"Go around, dunzy!" I shouted, but when I looked in the rearview mirror, I saw that the driver wore a pointy hat. The clurichaun grinned like a madman and tapped my back bumper. We shot forward. I wanted to stab that lep in the eye with his pointy hat.

The lep on the hood bashed his head against the windshield. A small crack began to spiderweb across the glass.

"You really messed up, Jack," Oswald said. "Admit it."

"I admit nothing, marshmallow."

"You didn't have to eat that leprechaun."

"I can't help myself. I'm a zombie."

"You're only a zombie if you believe you're a zombie. You can rise above it."

"Don't give me that pansy talk. Try not being a homunculus."

"I'm not a homunculus. I'm Oswald."

"Oh, jeez."

Blood dripped from the fairy's forehead as he continued to bash it against the windshield.

"Jack, do something," Oswald said.

"What are you doing, besides looking pretty?"

I cut a sharp right and the clurichaun blew past us. I cut another sharp right, and then a left, and came to a screeching halt in front of an abandoned warehouse. I knew the clurichaun would be back on us any minute so I had to work fast.

"Let's settle this like men," I said to my windshield fairy.

"That's what I like to hear," the lep said. "I'm going to grind you up into cat food. I'm going to make an ogre soup out of you."

"You're not going to fight him, are you, Jack?" Oswald said. "You haven't won a fight since you fought that blind, legless werewolf, and he still managed to rip off your right cheek."

"Always the confidence booster, Oswald, but don't worry, because *you're* going to take care of this half a kook."

"You can't be serious?"

I glared at Oswald. He knew when I meant business.

"Ain't you got a Napoleon complex, dunzy? Show this guy what you're made of!"

"I'm fine with my size and abilities."

"Get out of the car, Oswald!" To the lep, I said, "He's much tougher than he looks."

Oswald, ever the trouper, opened the door and stepped out. The lep hopped off the hood, stood in the street, and put up his dukes. Like I said, he was a real stereotype and, like a real stereotype, he was predictable. I threw the car into reverse and hit the gas.

"Stupid leprechaun!" I shouted.

Oswald quickly picked up on what I was doing—you gotta be fast to work with Dead Jack—and leapt back into the car.

"Good thinking," Oswald said.

"Thank me when we're back at the office."

We lost the lep, and I turned onto Water Street, going about ninety miles an hour, thinking what a smart zombie I was, when I ran smack into the clurichaun's car. Fortunately, I slammed into the driver's-side door. The red fairy was wearing an "oh fookin hell" expression as I pinned his vehicle against a parked hearse. The clurichaun didn't move, clearly stunned.

One advantage to being a zombie and a homunculus: we don't stun.

But the Studebaker was totaled. So, we did the only thing we could. We ran.

I began my power-shambling bit and Oswald jumped on my shoulder. "We need to get out of ShadowShade," he said. "Let this cool down for a while."

"You know I don't care for traveling abroad. Pandemonium's other four cities are the sticks."

"No alternative. Head to the dock. We'll catch a boat."

"I don't do boats."

"Do you do angry leprechauns? If this gets back to Dana, there will be a bounty on your head."

"That may be preferable to the Broken Sea."

"I hear the ships have nice accommodations these days. All-you-can-eat buffets, chocolate towers, little mints on your pillow."

"The only accommodation I need is not drowning."

"You'll be fine, you big, dead baby."

3

SHIP OF FOOLS

We waded through thick, fat plumes of fog searching for signs of life along the dock, but we didn't see so much as a ghost rat. A buoy clanged somewhere out in the Broken Sea. I watched the black water with dread. It looked like a giant graveyard. My greatest fear is drowning. My second greatest fear is *not* drowning and being trapped in the Broken Sea forever. When you can't die, you need to choose your surroundings carefully.

"Over here!" Oswald shouted.

I was too busy imagining my watery death to notice the ship docked to my left. It was huge, though most of it was hidden by the mist. It was one of those wooden jobs with jibs and masts and sails and whatever else old ships have. Fog curled around the vessel. I couldn't see if anyone was aboard. No lights burned. I sure didn't hear anyone.

"Where are these luxury ships you were talking about?" I said.

"They must all be out cruising the high seas."

"Why do I listen to you? I'm holding you responsible for this."

"Right! I devoured a leprechaun in Irish Town! I have a dust addiction!"

"You're a judgmental little thing, aren't you, Oswald?"

"You need to kick this dust habit once and for all."

"Then I'd be devouring everyone I come across, like every other two-bit zombie in Pandemonium."

"You're not like the other zombies in Pandemonium, Jack."

"Look, if I could, I'd take dust every day, but I don't. That has to count for something."

"I'd be happier if you were totally clean."

"You would, huh? Come here."

I grabbed Oswald.

"What are you doing?" he asked but didn't try to get away. The little creep gets a thrill when I touch him.

"I'm going to throw you onto the deck so you can find a rope and toss it to me."

"You don't have to do that. I can jump up there myself."

"I'd rather toss you. It'll make me feel like I'm contributing."

"Can you see in this fog?"

"Is that a zombie crack, wise guy?"

"What's being a zombie have to do with it?"

"Poor eyesight is a zombie stereotype. I happen to have perfect vision."

"I just mean it's foggy."

"We're wasting time."

Oswald rolled up into a ball for aerodynamic purposes. (The little bugger gets on my nerves, but his shape-shifting abilities do come in handy.) I reared back and chucked him. He smacked into the side of the ship with a nice *thump.*

"You did that on purpose!" Oswald said after he jumped out of the water and onto the railing of the top deck.

"I guess it was too foggy for me to see with my zombie eyes. Sorry, pal."

"You're going to be sorry when I'm not around to get you out of trouble."

"Oswald, find a damn rope so I can hang you."

The homunculus jumped off the railing and disappeared. He returned a moment later carrying a rope, which he had anchored to a mast and tossed down to me. I climbed up. Zombies have strong arms. Otherwise we'd never be able to dig ourselves out of our graves. (That's a joke. I never climbed out of a grave. If I had ever been buried, I'd probably never leave my comfy coffin.)

As I expected, no one roamed the deck. The ship was quieter than Oswald's brain. I could now see the sails were in tatters, torn and full of holes, as if they had been bombarded by a thousand cannonballs. The deck creaked with every step we took on the rotten, moss-covered floorboards.

"Looks like you picked the worst ship in ShadowShade, Oswald."

"Let's go below deck. We can hide out there, rest up, and in the morning find another ship that's leaving the city."

I had no intention of sailing the Broken Sea. I was glad this ship was unseaworthy. In the morning, I'd figure something out or just go back to my Midtown office. I've dealt with angry fairies before.

We headed to the lower decks. The rest of the ship was just as quiet and dark as the dock. Good thing Oswald can glow. I followed the homunculus through empty cabins. The stench of rot and decay pervaded everything in the vessel. But, oddly, there were no rats. Even they had abandoned the ship. We found a comfy spot in a cargo room, which was mostly bare, except for a few barrels. Empty barrels, unfortunately. I could have gone for some rum-spiked formaldehyde.

"Oswald," I said, "you take first shift. Make sure no one sneaks up on us."

"Sure thing, boss."

Oswald stood at the door, hands on his hips like some ragdoll sentinel. At least it would keep his mouth shut. Besides, he snores.

I curled up against a barrel, pulled my fedora over my face, and closed my eyes.

Sooner than I expected, I was in zombie dreamland. It's not a pleasant place. Why couldn't I dream of brains like the typical walking dead?

I'm back in Room 731. Still alive. But not for long.

I'm strapped to a steel chair this time. Naked. I want to scream, but my throat is paralyzed. My heart beats in my ears, and I fear a heart attack. But then I realize that would be a blessing.

A face covered in a surgical mask dominates my field of vision. I can hear his breath—hard and deep—through the covering.

He smells of tobacco and witch hazel. He has different-colored eyes. One blue-white, the other nearly black. Heterochromia. I remember him telling me that's what it's called. I can't stop staring at those eyes. With all the terrible things that have happened to me in this room, those eyes scare me more than anything. He's a doctor and a psychopath. He holds a clipboard and writes furiously on it. He stares at me as if trying to read my inner thoughts, and then scribbles away.

The fucked-up eyes get closer, just inches from my own. The mad doctor shines a penlight in my eyes and again records something on his clipboard.

"Specimen 1-1-3-4," he says from behind his mask. "You are in for a treat today." He motions to one of his assistants, who approaches with a red tin can. I instantly recognize it. A gas can.

I struggle in my restraints.

"Are you still afraid after all this time?" the voice behind the mask asks. "It will behoove you to remain calm!" His voice rises. Through gritted teeth, the psychopath says, "The entire procedure depends on you remaining calm!"

The assistant pours the gasoline over my head. I expect it to be hot, but it's ice cold. It gets in my eyes and my mouth. The sweet, metallic smell overwhelms me and makes me light-headed. I'm anything but calm.

The mad doctor walks over to a steel table and picks up a pack of Lucky Strikes. He removes his mask. His little Hitler mustache does a poor job of hiding his cleft palate.

The assistant has hightailed it to the far end of the room.

From his pants pocket, the Nazi doctor removes a lighter

emblazoned with a big, red swastika and lights the Lucky. He takes a long drag.

"Your American cigarettes are much better than the Russian's," he says as he blows smoke at me.

"I'd bum a smoke from you," I say, "but I figure they're hazardous to my health, considering I'm covered in gasoline."

The doctor doesn't laugh. "I see you haven't lost your sense of humor. That is excellent. We are making progress." He writes on his clipboard.

"If you can't laugh, then what have you got, right?"

"You are a real—what's the word? Cow-boy. Like your famous John Wayne."

"I'm more a Buster Crabbe fan."

"Yes. The Buck Rogers."

"I'd go with Flash Gordon. But whatever floats your boat."

The doctor flicks the Lucky at me and I go up like a garbage fire. My skin sizzles like bacon fat and melts. Indescribable pain racks my body. I scream, but again nothing comes out of my mouth. I'm thrashing wildly and manage to lift the chair. It topples over. How's that for calm?

Even with the flames crackling and burning me alive, I swear I can hear the psycho scribbling on his clipboard.

At some point, I black out. It's the fourth, maybe fifth time I've died in Room 731. This is the worst one, so far. But I know what's to come.

As I drift off into the dream darkness, I hear a voice. "Hallo, mein cow-boy." I know with certainty this isn't part of the dream. "It has taken me many years, 1-1-3-4," the voice says, "but I am getting close. I am closer than you think." In the *darkness, eyes—blue-white and black—appear.*

I scream and this time I hear it.

I awoke like it was another one of my resurrections, thinking I could feel my heart banging against my chest. I don't even know if I have a heart anymore. I certainly don't have a soul.

I sat up in the cargo room, shaking.

He was dead, wasn't he? How could he be in Pandemonium? Lucifer, no! The voice echoed in my head. *1-1-3-4. 1-1-3-4.* I reached for a hellfire stick but remembered the dream, saw him flicking that Lucky Strike at me. I pulled my hand back and ran it over my face. My ugly, hideous face.

It had been a rough day. It was just a dream. I needed to get a grip.

Bang! Bang! Bang!

It wasn't my heart. It came from above. Stupid Oswald was asleep, curled up against me and snoring like an asthmatic chicken. So much for the little sentinel.

Bang! Bang! Bang!

I knocked on Oswald's head.

"Was that you?" I said.

"Was what me?" Oswald said. I wondered if he dreamed, but the dope was probably too simple for that.

"That banging."

"I was sleeping."

"Weren't you supposed to be guarding us?"

Bang! Bang! Bang! It sounded like a pack of ogres doing the Charleston.

"The leps found us," Oswald whispered.

"Those aren't leps. Wait! Do you hear that?"

"I don't hear anything. What?"

"See? Zombie hearing is superior. It's music, dunzy." I could see Oswald straining to hear, but he couldn't. The twerp doesn't even have ears. "Go up there and take a look around."

"Why me?"

"Because, Oswald, you are as insignificant and indistinct as a blob of candle wax. No one will notice you."

"You're afraid."

"Have I ever been afraid of anything?"

"The ogre Madgogg, spiders, water, not having enough dust."

"You're a broken record. Quit nagging already."

"No."

"I gave up eating people. Mostly. I can't give up dust, too. It's fine. It's medicinal."

"The dust messes up your mind."

"Like when you took up residence in my skull?"

"I apologized for that."

"I don't feel like you were truly sorry."

"I'm sorry you're stalling because you're afraid of what's above us."

"You are one step closer to being demoted. Watch it, marshmallow. What does a man who has overcome death itself have to fear, homunculus? I am a member of the soulless. I—"

Now if Oswald were to tell it, he would say I shrieked like a pixie whose wings were being plucked off. But it wasn't like that at all. I was merely trying to scare off the mouse that had leapt from the shadows to attack me. It must have been a vampire mouse. Its fangs were huge and sharp. Had it gotten up my pant leg, it could have done some real damage. Vermin and walking corpses don't mix.

My shriek worked. The mouse scampered off. Oswald tried his best to suppress a laugh. I would have thrown him overboard, but I wouldn't give him the satisfaction.

"On second thought," I said, "I will go with you, since you'll probably mess things up."

When we exited the cargo room, the music grew louder. "That's not leprechaun music," I said. It was more nautical and dark and—if possible—more drunken.

The music wasn't our only problem, though. The ship wasn't as unseaworthy as I had thought. I looked out a grimy porthole and watched black water crash against the hull. We could have been halfway across the Broken Sea by now.

"I don't think this ship is as abandoned as you thought," Oswald said.

"Thank you, Mr. Obvious."

We crept through the ship. I kept my eyes on the ground, ready for another vampire mouse attack. No one seemed to be below deck. All the action was happening up top. I didn't like it one bit.

When we reached the ladder leading to the top deck, Oswald tried to go up first but I pushed him out of the way. I'd show him I wasn't afraid. At the top of the ladder, I carefully opened the hatch and peeked out. Even with my zombie vision, I knew exactly who was manning this ship.

Instruments blared and haunted voices sang under the red sky of Pandemonium.

"Nice going, Oswald, you put us on a ghost pirate ship!"

Dozens of spirits crowded the upper deck. They pulled on ropes, adjusted sails, and swabbed the deck, all while making merry. Some sat on the rail with jugs of rum, while others groggily swayed back and forth. Barrels thumped and rolled. Someone kept sounding a damn gong. *Bong! Bong! Bong!* It gave me the heebie-jeebies.

The ship glided through the water as smoothly as a vampire's fangs through a virgin's neck.

"What are we going to do?" Oswald said.

I tapped my chest. "*The Book of the Three Towers*," I said. But when I went to pull it out of my jacket pocket, it wasn't there. "Fook! I forgot the grimoire back at the office."

"Great!"

"No worries. I have that thing practically memorized."

"Practically?"

I climbed onto the deck, stood, dusted off my clothes, and adjusted my fedora to a rakish angle. I cleared my considerably clotted throat and racked my brain for the grimoire's section on ghost pirates, or was it pirate ghosts? I remembered a bit about water spirits and another about undead *primates*, but that probably wouldn't help. It would come to me, though.

"Infernal creatures of the night," I began. "Spectators of the sea—I mean *specters* of the sea. Heed my words." I held out my arms.

The ghost party continued.

Yo, ho, yo, ho!
Yo, ho, yo, ho!
Yo, ho, yo, ho!
They sang louder. The barrels thumped harder.

I moved to the center of the ship. "O spirits of the depths, I commend you—"

"Don't you mean *command* you?" Oswald said.

"Right. I command you to, to—" To Oswald, I whispered, "What do I want to command them to do?"

Oswald shrugged.

A spirit with a large gold earring in his left ear swooped down from atop one of the sails and hovered above me. He had only one eye, which was swollen and red. Big chunks of his beard were missing and he seemed to have only one tooth to go with his one eye. He gave Oswald and me the once over. I could see the moon and black clouds right through him.

"Are you the captain of this blasted ship?" I asked.

The ghost didn't answer but, after a moment, he whistled and the music died. The ship creaked and water crashed against the hull. A large spirit rose from the forecastle and floated toward me. The other ghosts moved out of his way as he approached.

The specter, pale and tall, wore a wide-brimmed hat and a long black coat. A rusty cutlass hung at his side. Some may have called him a handsome fella, young and blue eyed, but that was the left side of his face. The right looked as if a rat had used it as a chew toy. Inflamed flesh drooped in ragged strips. His right ear was just a nub. A little creature sat on his shoulder. I didn't know if it was a devil or a monkey. Its body was smooth and red as hellfire, and its face resembled that of a primate, except it had no skin. It wore no clothing other than a hat adorned with a skull and crossbones.

The mutilated pirate leaned in close to me and studied me like he was trying to figure out the answer to a difficult question.

"Ain't never heard a revenant speak before," he said.

"I'm full of surprises," I said.

"Stowaways, sir," the first ghost said.

"Are you the captain?" I asked. "I'd like to know if I'm talking to the spirit in charge."

"I am Captain Louis F. Schroeder, the scourge of the Broken Lands, the raider of the Broken Sea, the scallywag of the depths. But most people call me Captain Half-Face."

"Sorry about the stowaway business, Louie. We didn't know this ship was *ocupado*. You ghosts are pretty sneaky on that front, aren't you? If you'd kindly drop us off on the nearest island, we'll be on our way."

The pirate stroked his ratty blond half-of-beard. The devil monkey refused to make eye contact with me. It kept its head bowed. "Certainly," the captain said. "I don't see any problem with that. You made an honest mistake. Could happen to any of us."

I shot Oswald a look. He seemed relieved. The little guy can get quite nervous. "Reasonable ghost pirates," I said. "That's a welcome change of pace. You have restored my faith in Pandemonium, sir." I gave a little bow.

"Can I get you two any refreshments?" Captain Louie said. "Beer? Grog? Sardines?"

"If you have any Devil Boy, I wouldn't mind a pint."

"Do you have a chocolate tower?" Oswald said, and I kicked him.

The little monkey devil whispered in Captain Louie's ear. The pirate listened, his eyebrows knitting together. Every now and then he'd nod in seeming agreement or laugh. The runt really chewed his ear off. (Not literally, though I was pretty sure he was responsible for Captain Half-Face's half a face.)

Finally, the creature stopped jabbering and Captain Louie said, "He's shy."

The devil monkey again cast his eyes down.

"So how about that formaldehyde?" I said. "I imagine you fellas partake as well. Never mind the homunculus. He's not used to ghost pirates."

"Actually," Captain Louie said, "Ned doesn't want to drop you and your friend off. He wants us to kill you both."

I coughed. Maybe I gagged. I'm not certain.

"Ned?" I pointed at the monkey. "He's Ned?"

"He's not usually like this, but he makes a great point."

"He does, does he? And what's his point?"

"He reminded me that *The Phantom Clipper* cannot stop until we've destroyed the red beast."

"The red beast?"

"*The Phantom Clipper* has only one mission: to find the Red Kraken and kill it, as Ned here kindly reminded me."

"In roaring, he shall rise and on the surface die," a spirit said.

"Aye, every night we awaken and pick up the chase," another called out.

"Do whatever you need to do at night," I said. "We don't mind. You can drop us off in the morning."

Ned whispered in Captain Louie's ear again. He nodded and agreed. "Ned says he's changed his mind. We don't have to kill you."

"I'm glad he came to his senses. Thank you, Ned." I bowed before the monkey devil, but he turned his back on me.

Captain Louie drew his sword and pointed it at us. "Lash the soulless one to the prow!" he commanded.

Three ghosts swooped out of the air and pounced on me. Before I could protest, my hands were pinned behind my back.

Oswald rushed the ghosts, but they grabbed him. They weren't so incorporeal when they needed to be.

They all began chanting, "Kraken bait! Kraken bait! Kraken bait!"

"And this wee creature," the captain said, nodding to Oswald, "toss him overboard." And that's just what they did. The homunculus went sailing over the side of the ship. I didn't even hear the splash. The ship just went zipping through the water.

"You didn't need to do that!" I shouted. "Sure, he's annoying, but—"

They gagged me and then I was dragged toward the front of the ship. I tried kicking the spirits, but my leg went through them. They dangled me over the water, and I made the mistake of looking down. The Broken Sea crashed against the ship and sprayed me. I think I screamed.

4

KRAKEN BAIT

I've never liked ghosts. You can't trust them. They always have some gripe or mission or obsession. Shadow-Shade is full of spirits, hence the name, so I know what I'm talking about. My secretary, Lilith, is a specter. She's always going on about being hammered to death. Let it go, honey. It happened centuries ago. But ghosts can't let anything go. A kraken? A damn kraken? What the hell were they going after a sea monster for?

I had never seen one of the beasts before. I was sure I didn't want to. At least they weren't hunting Cthulhu.

They had tied me to the prow like a hog on a spit. The bad music and dancing started up again. It was a real ghost pirate dance party. But now it wasn't such a fun, celebratory bash. It was more ominous and sinister.

They sang:

"Below the thunders of the upper deep,

Far, far beneath in the abysmal sea..."

Someone kept sounding that fookin gong. My stomach churned and my head pounded in sync with the clanging. *Bong! Bong! Bong!* I fell into a stupor and had nearly nodded off when the sea began to boil. The black water swelled, the waves rising and tossing. Something inside my guts swelled and churned. I readied myself to puke, but nothing came up.

The Broken Sea crashed all around me, soaking my poor suit. I rubbed the back of my head against the prow to push my fedora farther down. It was the only one I had. I could take losing Oswald, but not my hat. Why did I ever listen to that runt?

The pirates continued their chanting.

Wave upon wave besieged *The Phantom Clipper*. The ship rolled and pitched. I swallowed what must have been a gallon of seawater.

The ghost vessel climbed a swell and continued heading up, up, up the expanding sea wall. The beast rose from the depths, pulling the water toward the sky. Its dead, black eyes appeared first, and then its lumpy pink-red head. It was as if the Empire Snake Building was emerging from the sea. Soon, tentacles, fat and bloated, writhed in all directions like an army of giant snakes. Suckers the size of Studebakers. Its skin shined with an otherworldly glow.

The kraken was only fifty yards from the ship and we were heading straight for it. It slapped it tentacles at the water, first playfully, and then ruthlessly. A tidal wave sped toward *The Phantom Clipper* and I was right in the line of fire. The water punched me like a thunderbolt thrown by Zeus himself, and the ship flew a hundred feet into the air. When we crashed back down, I got another mouthful of saltwater.

Captain Louie now stood above me, shouting at the sea monster.

"In roaring, he shall rise and on the surface die!"

"Pipe down," I said. "He might hear you, dunzy!"

The rest of the crew took up the chant. The devil monkey chittered and hopped up and down on the captain's shoulder.

"In roaring, he shall rise and on the surface die!"

"In roaring, he shall rise and on the surface die!"

"In roaring, he shall rise and on the surface die!"

"You can let me go now!" I shouted. "The kraken's here, you don't need me anymore!"

The captain ignored me and hurled an obsidian spear at the beast. The kraken swatted it away like it was a twig. The ship rocked and rolled on fifty-foot waves. Water crashed all around us, but I could still hear that stupid gong. Others tried their hand at the spear-throwing. They rained down projectiles on the sea beast. The kraken swatted them all away with little effort. Was that all they had? After all this time, their only plan was to throw sticks at the thing?

When the kraken tired of batting spears, he batted *The Phantom Clipper*. A tentacle, like a giant pink tongue, rose, blocked out the moon, and came crashing down the middle of the ship. The *Clipper* tried its best, but the poor thing had no other choice than to split in half. Beams and masts and sails exploded from the ship and sank into the sea. But the kraken was just getting started. Tentacles flew in a whirlwind. All I saw were red streaks and bits of the ship tumbling into the sea. Ever hear a ghost scream? It's not something you'll soon forget. I only ever heard something worse in Room 731.

The water devil was determined to reduce *The Phantom Clipper* to a toothpick. And even that toothpick was probably going to be smashed.

Eventually the prow, with me still lashed to it, broke off and fell into the churning water. At least I no longer heard that damn gong.

I don't know what happened to the ghost pirates. Maybe without the ship, they disappeared, the boat acting like some battery giving them existence. I'm sure they weren't harmed.

As for me? The bastards tied me well. Damn pirates are good with knots. Even ghost ones.

The prow eventually bobbed to the surface of the water. Unfortunately, I was on the underside, still submerged in the Broken Sea. This was it, I thought, stuck in the bloody drink forever. Thank you, Oswald! Ever since I hooked up with that damn homunculus I've had nothing but misery and annoyance. "You're taking too much dust, Jack." "You're not a zombie if you don't act like one, Jack." "Don't eat that fairy, Jack."

I was beginning to get waterlogged, when I finally spun myself around.

I wasn't completely uncomfortable riding atop that prow as it bobbed and rocked through the water. It did wonders for my back. As the hours rolled by, I amused myself by planning my revenge. I figured I'd hire a team of mystics, if I ever got back to ShadowShade, and hold a huge séance. Once all the spirits were conjured, I'd force them all to listen to my gong solo till the end of time. I was going to use that Ned as my mallet. What was that runt's deal?

Something moved along the surface of the water. I didn't have much range of vision. I could turn slightly to the left and right, but I didn't see anything. The prow rose over a swell and when I reached the crest, I spotted a fin—a sharp, gray fin curved like a scimitar. I watched as it circled me.

Now there are many things in the Broken Sea besides krakens. You have your ghost dolphins, your whalewolves, devil porpoises, hydras, terrible dogfish, mega-jellyfish, mermaids and mermen, kelpies, selkies, sea hags, dinocrocs, Cthulhu, and satanic sea monkeys. The water is probably the worst place in Pandemonium where you could find yourself. Which is right where I found myself. Lucky me.

This wasn't a ghost shark, since the fin was solid. That left one thing: a shark woman!

The most important thing to know about shark women is that there are no shark men. These fishy females are always on the hunt for a mate, and here I was, an incapacitated, black-blooded male. Easy pickings for a shark woman.

She continued to circle, the fin getting closer with each revolution. I worked my jaw. If she was going to eat me, I was going to do my best to eat her. A bite for a bite. I'm not usually a fan of seafood, but I could make an exception. After three circles, the fin disappeared.

Maybe she went away, realized I wasn't such a good catch after all. I wasn't the sort of guy anyone brought home to their mother, even as a meal.

No such luck.

The shark woman roared up from the depths and torpedoed into the prow, sending me ten feet into the air. When I came down, I was again under the water with the prow above me. I caught a murky glimpse of the creature as she swam toward me. She had the arms and face of a woman. Some may have even called her beautiful, if you didn't mind the seaweed-colored hair and the gill slits beside her flat nose. Her lower half, though, was all shark. She smiled at me and all I could see were three rows of knife-like teeth.

The shark woman grabbed me and spun me back up to the surface. She then floated beside the prow. I didn't move. I heard the best way to deal with a shark woman is to remain perfectly still. They react to movement.

She shook me. I went limp.

"Are you dead or something?" she said.

If there's one thing I'm good at, it's playing dead.

The shark woman leaned over and kissed me on the lips.

I screamed.

"Hey, you're alive!"

"Technically, no," I said.

"A zombie?" She spit into the ocean as if she'd tasted something bad, like zombie lips.

"We don't make the best meals."

"What are you doing out here in the middle of the Broken Sea tied up like this? Are you into some weird bondage?"

"I ran into some ghost pirates, a devil monkey, and a kraken."

"Sounds like a hell of a sex party." The shark woman grinned.

"It had nothing to do with sex."

"That's a shame."

"Not from my perspective."

"From the looks of it, you could have used it."

"What's that supposed to mean?"

"You seem a bit uptight."

"Well, I was almost killed by a giant sea monster not too long ago."

"You were? You poor thing. You must be terrified." The shark woman hugged me.

"I'm good," I said. "You can let me go."

She slowly released me from her powerful grip and stroked my arm. "A strong man. I like that. Can I feel your muscles?"

This shark woman must have been out to sea a long while. She was creepier than a virgin satyr at a prom.

"Is it true there are no shark men?" I asked, trying to change the subject.

"Yes."

"Why is that?"

"We ate them all."

"Oh."

"Once we mate, we bite the heads off our lovers. It's our thing."

"And you didn't foresee a problem with eating your men?"

"We did. We just didn't care. Shark men are jerks."

"That sounds sexist."

"It is sexy."

"Not sexy. *Sexist.*"

"That's what I said. By the way, what's your sign?"

"I'm a cancer."

"I should have figured that."

"Would you mind untying me? I'd like to get back to land eventually. I'm not made for the sea."

"Oh, sure. I'm amphibian, if you were wondering. Where do you live? Maybe I'll come visit you."

She went to work on the ropes with her knife teeth. The ropes didn't stand a chance. When I was free, I slid off the prow and treaded water beside the shark woman.

"I move around a lot," I said. I didn't think it wise to give a shark woman my address.

"A traveling man, huh?'

"That's me. I never stay in one place too long and I'd rather not stay in this blasted water any longer. If it's not a bother, can you take me to shore?"

"What do I get in return?"

I was pretty sure I knew exactly what she wanted. "You can't have my head. How about we hold hands?"

"Is that as far as you're willing to go? I didn't know zombies were such prudes."

"Then I won't admit that your kiss was my first."

"Don't ever admit that. It's too sad. Jump on my back and I'll take you wherever you want to go. I'll think of something when we get to shore."

I slipped my arms around the shark woman.

"I'm Georgina, by the way."

"I'm Jack."

"Nice to meet you, Jack. Now hold on tight. I move fast."

"You don't say?"

Georgina took off like a gun blast and I almost slammed my face into her fin.

"Are you into yoga, Jack?" the shark woman said as she sped through the dark water.

"What?

"Yoga. Tantric yoga. I've been studying it. Pretty interesting stuff."

"I don't mess with my ligaments on account of me being a corpse."

"It might do you some good, Jack. Limber you up. Then you might not be such a prude." She flipped her tail up between my legs and giggled. If blood filled my veins, I would have blushed.

"You seem like a swell gal, but—"

I had a *but*, right? I searched my brain for it, but I couldn't find an excuse to rebuff the shark woman's advances. I didn't even have a good enough reason for her not to bite my head off. Maybe there was no *but*.

"There's someone else?" Georgina said. "You have an undead doll waiting for you on land?"

"Not exactly. I have a friend, a partner... He's more of an associate really."

"Oh?" she said with a weird accusatory rise in her voice.

"It's not like that. We work together."

"You two are close?"

"We used to be closer. He lived inside me for six months. Oh, that came out wrong."

"Sounds right to me."

"It isn't what you're thinking. He took up residence in a hollow part of my skull, without my permission, I may add."

"Sounds like a kinky little guy. You two still together?"

"We're not together. I've tried many times to get rid of him, but I can never shake him."

"Sounds like you're in denial, honey."

I was about to say something, but I just let out a sigh. How can I explain Oswald? He's unexplainable.

After a few awkward moments of silence, I spotted land, thank Lucifer.

Georgina bounced off the waves like a satanic sea monkey pursuing a sinner as she raced toward the beach at Coney Island. When she ran out of water, she dove and slid onto the sand. I went tumbling off the shark woman and crash-landed on a carpet of broken shells.

I stood and watched the shark woman rise onto her two back fins. She waddled over to me.

"Where's your friend now?" she said.

"I didn't say he was a friend."

"Okay, you're not in denial."

"He's gone."

"You two broke up?" She smiled, clearly having fun with me now.

"I'm not going to say it again."

"Lighten up, Jack. You really should try that tantric yoga."

"I have dust to keep me limber."

"That stuff will kill you."

"I'm hoping."

"If you're so hell-bent on being offed, we could mate."

"I do have something for you. Here's my card." I handed her a sopping wet business card from my wallet and she took it. It was probably a mistake, but I was warming to the shark woman.

"A detective, huh?"

"Not too many other jobs for guys like me. I take the cases no one else wants."

"I'll keep you in mind if I ever need a dick."

"Cute," I said and laughed. The shark woman winked. "You shark women aren't too bad, if you overlook the mass murdering stuff."

"If we mated, you wouldn't mind being murdered, honey. Believe me. I've never had any complaints. Think about it. Bye, Jack. I hope you find your...whatever he is."

And with that, Georgina dove back into the Broken Sea and swam off.

I dropped onto the sand exhausted. I planned on taking a quick rest, but I fell asleep as soon as my head touched the ground. Fortunately, I had a dreamless sleep. No Room 731, thank Lucifer. I thought things were looking up, until a curious goblin awoke me with a kick to the face.

5

DOWN AND OUT
IN THE BROKEN LANDS

The goblin smiled, exposing yellow-green teeth. I knew a demented dentist who could clean that infernal plaque, but the goblin wasn't getting any referrals from me.

If the Broken Sea is the deadliest place in Pandemonium, the Broken Lands run a close second. The place was home to all manner of nasties, especially demons and vampires. The terrain was rocky and full of fires—oh boy, were there ever fires—and lava. Lots of flowing lava. The city is the most hellish of the hells in Pandemonium, which is saying something.

I rubbed my jaw where the goblin kicked it and watched two other goblins appear. I tried to sit up, but it wasn't going to happen. I fell back on the sand with a thump. Seaweed covered most of my body. My dry cleaner will be able to put both his kids through wizard school with my bill.

One of the goblins jumped on my chest and took a seat. The black tufts of hair sticking out of his pointy ears were kind of gross. Grosser than his yellow, bloodshot eyes.

"Comfy?" I asked.

I tried pushing him off, but my arms didn't want to work.

The goblin reached into the inside pocket of my jacket and pulled out my wallet. One second in the Broken Lands and I was being mugged. He opened it, most likely checking for cash, which of course wasn't there.

"Are things that bad in the Broken Lands that you guys have to mug shipwrecked zombies?"

The goblin jumped onto its clawed feet and hopped up and down like a Mexican jumping bean on dust. He yelled something to his compatriots in the goblin language. They ran over to him and he handed them my card. Who knew goblins liked business cards?

I lay on the sand a moment groaning in pain. Man, had I taken a beating. I tried sitting up again. I got there, but I immediately fell back down. I had never wanted a hit of dust worse than at that moment. I reached for my pack of Lucky Dragons. They were soaked. I tried to wring out one hellfire stick, but it was hopeless. Well, third time's the charm. I slowly rose, heard a few *pops* in my back, and sat up.

The goblins stood before me, their eyes wide.

I played it cool, waiting for them to get close. I've had goblin before and it's some of the toughest meat around. I tried loosening my jaw.

The goblin who pinched my wallet shouted, "Dead Jack, the goblin queen seeks your presence!"

"Goblin queen, huh?" It seemed a bit queer that anyone here would seek my presence when I had just dropped in, but I had nothing better to do.

The goblin helped me to my feet. The two other goblins stood at my sides and propped me up. Together, like a four-headed crab, we inched our way toward the woods just beyond the beach.

"Any reason why your goblin queen wants to see me?" I asked.

The goblins had lost their chattiness. They wouldn't answer any of my questions or even tell me their names.

The trio led me through the woods until we came to a cave. By then, I could walk a bit, but with the way I was shuffling I looked like a biter right off the boat from the Zombie Islands.

I entered the cave on my own. The goblins ran ahead, shouting, "Dead Jack! Dead Jack! Dead Jack!" The goblins leapt about and bounced off the walls, where torches flickered in niches. Their thin arms flailed in the air. They were like little kids on Christmas morning.

I could have headed back out of the cave and away from the goblins, but I was curious about this goblin queen. I had never met royalty before.

Shadows danced on the walls and the sound of dripping water echoed in the chamber. As I followed the goblins, I noticed we were heading farther underground. The air grew colder and damper. It didn't help that I was soaking wet. I was going to be the first zombie to die of pneumonia.

Finally, we came to a wooden door with a big brass ring in the center. The goblins had settled down, no more funny business. The first goblin pulled on the ring and carefully opened the door. He bowed his head, as did the other two goblins. I walked through the door after I pulled off all the bits of seaweed from my suit and adjusted my hat to the proper angle. I wanted to make a good impression. The goblins stayed behind.

I might have entered a palace. The place was lavish even by Upper West Side ShadowShade standards. I saw sapient fainting couches with silk massaging hands and elvish rugs woven with gold threads and diamond chandeliers that glittered like fairy dust in the sun. The light glinted off obsidian statues of griffins and phoenixes and sphinxes. Paintings depicting moments in Pandemonium's history hung on the walls. One showed the first great battle between werewolves and fairies that gave the Red Garden its name. Ferocious wolves in shiny armor tore through ranks of fairies equipped only with pointy hats and shoes. The red came mostly from the wee folk.

A goblin in trousers, a red velvet smoking jacket, and ascot stood in front of a large gilded mirror. I had never seen a goblin wearing clothes. Maybe that was because this fella owned all the apparel in the Broken Lands. Beside the mirror were racks and racks of every type of fashion imaginable: from togas and zoot suits to hoop skirts and tuxedos. The goblin was no taller than Oswald. How did I know that? Because Oswald was standing right next to him.

Oswald wore a white suit with red ascot. At the moment, he was trying on a floppy hat, which he positioned at different angles while checking himself out in the mirror.

"I prefer the one with the red feather," the clothed goblin said.

"I don't know," Oswald said. "I think this one works better with my head shape. It's so hard to find a well-fitted hat these days."

They were too busy to notice me so I cleared my throat. The two well-dressed shrimps pried themselves from the mirror and turned.

"Putting on a play?" I asked.

"Jack!" Oswald said.

"You're like a bad penny, Oswald. You keep coming back."

"I told the goblins to keep an eye out for you. I figured you'd wash up sooner or later."

"You look ridiculous, by the way."

"I think I look swell," Oswald said as he placed his hands on his hips and cocked his head to the side.

"These clothes come from the finest elvish tailors in Pandemonium," the goblin said.

"Oswald, you look like a milkman with a bleeding goiter," I said. "Take off the suit."

"Are you the only one in the relationship allowed to wear clothes?" the goblin asked me.

"We don't have a relationship."

"See?" Oswald said to the goblin. "This is what I've been telling you."

"He does seem to have issues," the goblin said.

"I don't know why I put up with it."

"What have you been telling this guy?" I asked the homunculus.

The goblin's bat-like ears shot straight up. "I am a *queen*, you dead dolt!"

"Never seen any queen dress like you."

"How many queens have you seen?"

"Counting you? One."

The queen turned to Oswald and said, "I really do not see how this *zombie* can be of help to the goblin nation. He seems a perfect idiot, and a terribly dressed one at that. Were you buried in that suit?"

"What makes you think I was buried? Don't believe everything you hear about zombies."

"Well, I believe that suit should be put out of its misery. Burn it so it has no chance of being resurrected."

"I don't need this abuse," I said. "Come on, Oswald. Let's scram."

"Wait, Jack. The queen has a job for us."

"Not interested. I'm retired."

"When did you retire?"

"The moment I was tossed into the Broken Sea. I'm going to live out my days in rest and relaxation far from leprechauns and water."

"The queen needs our help, Jack."

"I'm leaving. If you want to stay, be my guest. You seem very comfortable here."

"Oswald, I don't see how your *friend* can help us," the royal said. "He doesn't seem to have a brain cell left in his thick skull."

I had enough and began to walk out of the goblin queen's boudoir. Beside the door something caught my eye. A golden bowl on a golden table. It was full of rainbow-colored powder.

"Is this fairy dust?" I asked.

"Jack!" Oswald shouted.

I stopped and turned to the goblin queen.

"The goblin nation is the number-one supplier of dust in the Broken Lands," she said.

I was warming to this cross-dressing goblin. "Out of curiosity, what's the job?"

"The goblins' cats are missing," Oswald said.

I don't work with animals, not unless you count Oswald. But... the dust.

"Why do you have cats?" I asked. "You eat them or dress them in tuxedos for laughs?"

"Felines are sacred to us," the goblin queen said. "They are our companions."

"I never cared much for cats myself."

"They're incredibly attuned creatures. I might say they are the most magical of all the beings in Pandemonium."

"How many cats are we talking here?"

"Fifty-two black cats," Oswald said.

"That's not much to go on. All the cats in Pandemonium are black."

"They started going missing about three months ago," Oswald said. "No one has ever seen it happen. They just vanish and are never seen again."

"Probably just some hungry demons. You got lots of them in the Broken Lands. Why don't you find them yourselves? You know this area better than we do?"

"You've met some of the goblins, haven't you?" the goblin queen said. "They're not the most reliable creatures."

I nodded.

"Jack can find your cats, Your Grace," Oswald said. "I make a solemn vow to you."

The goblin queen stroked her silk ascot. She looked at Oswald. "I have faith in you, Oswald," she said. "I can see you have spirit. I'm not too sure about your friend, but if the two of you can return our cats, the goblin nation will be eternally in your debt."

"Two kilos of dust a day, plus expenses," I said.

"Agreed." She responded so quickly I kicked myself for not asking for more.

"First two days payable now. And Oswald loses the suit. He looks like a dwarf pimp."

6

THE BEST-LAID PLAN

"**Do you have a plan?**" Oswald asked with an irritating, little man with a chip on his shoulder tone.

We walked across the burning plains of the Broken Lands, heading north. The goblin queen had said the cats liked to do their business there, though they never went much farther than a few yards from the border of Goblin Town. Smoke emanated from the innumerable fissures that crisscrossed the ash-covered ground. Everything was dead as far as the eye could see. Black and featureless, except for the orange-red glow on the horizon. That came from the Really Big Pit of Fire. The Broken Lands were filled with big fires, but this one, well, it was *really* big. It's probably been burning since the creation of Pandemonium. I'd meant to torch Oswald's suit there, but I couldn't wait. As soon as we left the goblin's cave, I had him disrobe. I shoved the suit in a crack in the ground and the thing went up in flames. Those threads were a fire hazard. I did him a favor.

"I have a plan," I said.

"Is it the first plan that entered your dust-addled head? The simplest, dumbest, most dangerous plan you could come up with?"

"It's a good plan. I think you're going to be surprised."

I shook out a wet hellfire stick from my pack and tried to light it, but it was tough going.

"Let's try something different this time," Oswald said. "Let's brainstorm. We'll bounce a few ideas off each other, see what sticks, huh?"

I got the tip of the Lucky Dragon to glow a bit, but it fizzled out. I tossed it on the ground and put the lighter away.

"I already have a plan," I said.

"Yes, I know, but let's see if there's a *better* plan. You know, one that won't involve us getting throw in the sea or used as kraken bait."

I stopped and sat on a heap of orc bones. I took out another hellfire stick and blew on it, hoping I could dry it out.

"Sure, what do you propose we do?" I asked.

The glow of the Really Big Pit of Fire grew brighter. I could see licks of flame shooting into the sky. It felt a bit hotter here, too. I held up the hellfire stick in the hot air and shook it. I needed a drag if I was going to listen to Oswald.

The homunculus stood before me like he was a business executive presiding over a board meeting. "Okay," he said, "thank you for hearing me out, Jack. I think we should go canvassing for information. We knock on doors, we gather information. Find out what people around here know about these missing cats or who might benefit from taking them. First, though, we need to create a grid and move systematically. You can take the east and I'll take the west."

"Can you morph into a cat?"

"What?"

"I've never seen you change into a cat. I was wondering if you're capable."

"Of course I can change into a cat. That's not much of a challenge. Cats have pretty simple structures."

"Well, show me." I raised an eyebrow.

"I'm trying to come up with a plan here. You're messing with the brainstorming flow."

I glared at the homunculus and waved my still-sopping-wet hellfire stick at him. "Amuse me, shape-shifter."

"You're insane, you know that?"

"I know that."

Oswald stood there not doing anything. I raised my eyebrow higher.

"But then we get back to brainstorming, right?" he said.

"Absolutely."

Oswald's body bulged and contracted like a rubber accordion until he was a tight, dense sphere. Out of the sphere formed cat legs and a head and a tail, even whiskers. In a matter of seconds, Oswald had become a nearly perfect little kitty cat. I wanted to throw a ball of yarn at him.

"We don't even know if these cats were taken," he said while he slunk back and forth, getting used to his feline body. His tail whipped from side to side. "They could have just walked off, gotten tired of Goblin Town. Cats are pretty unpredictable. Maybe we just go on a scouting mission. Think like a cat. Where would a cat go?" Oswald pawed at the ground.

"You missed the most important part," I said.

"What's that?"

"All cats in Pandemonium are black, dunzy."

"So?"

"Roll around on the ground and cover yourself in the ashes."

"Come on, Jack."

Another raised eyebrow and Kitty Oswald dropped to the ground and rolled in the ash, getting himself good and dirty and, most importantly, black. When he stood back up, he was the spitting image of a Pandemonium pussycat.

"Not bad, Oswald. Good kitty." He smiled. He liked that. I think I heard a little purr. "Go scamper a little farther ahead. Frolic like a cat. Really sell it. Make me believe your name is Mr. Whiskers."

"The brainstorming is going well, isn't it?"

"I'm with you a hundred percent, and I think embodying a cat is really helping your thought process. You're on fire, Mr. Whiskers."

"I am, right?"

Oswald shot across the burning plain, showing off his cat-like reflexes. He leapt and slunk and pawed at the sky. He purred and preened. I thought he was about to cough up a hairball.

"Farther out!" I shouted and waved him off.

Oswald scampered deeper into the wasteland. When I could barely see him, he stopped and shouted, "I've contributed, but you're not brainstorming at all. You never even told me your plan. What is it?"

I lit the hellfire stick and it began to glow.

"I use you as bait!"

"Bait?"

Just then, a black, winged nightmare dropped out of the sky, grabbed Kitty Oswald in its talons, and shot off in the direction of the Really Big Pit of Fire.

That wasn't part of the plan. "Crap!" I shouted, mostly to myself. I hadn't thought of a flying cat-napper.

I took a drag on my hellfire stick and watched the giant flames of the pit dance and shake in the darkness like some devilish bonfire. I took a few more drags until I felt a bit warm inside, and then I took off as fast as I could in the direction of the ancient fires of the Broken Lands.

7

AND INTO THE FIRE

I **couldn't get up to full power-shamble speed, but I** was lurching in double time. I looked like a marionette controlled by a puppeteer with the shakes.

The Broken Lands didn't make running any easier. They call them the Broken Lands for a reason. The hard-packed ground was cracked and in pieces. With each step, I nearly went flying.

Soon, though, the plain gave way to lava pits and lakes of fire and hills of bones. It was a nice change of scenery. You don't mind piles of basilisk carcasses after seeing only a big, black nothing.

As I approached the Really Big Pit of Fire, the joint really heated up. I started sweating. I didn't know I could still do that.

The winged demon had long ago disappeared into the blood-red sky. It was the one hitch in my plan. You can't foresee everything. Live and learn. The dunzy wanted to canvass. No one was around!

Little purple creatures, lizards maybe, scampered along the ground. One stopped, looked at me, and spit. When the thick saliva hit the ground, it sizzled and a puff of smoke rose from where it landed. I made a mental note to stay away from those things.

I needed to think. I sat beside a lake of fire. I had only three more hellfire sticks. Crap! Then I remembered the dust. The heavenly, magical dust. Oswald would bitch about it since I had just fed on a leprechaun, but of course he wasn't here. Besides, I was doing it for him, wasn't I?

I took out a baggie. (The queen handed me a dozen when we left Goblin Town.) All colors of the rainbow twinkled in the powder like gems in a dwarf mine. It was like a living kaleidoscope. Just looking at it gave me a buzz. I took a quick hit and it was fookin paradise.

I watched as the lake of fire burned bright yellow, then red and blue. Like the dust itself, every color imaginable swirled in the fire as if a giant, drunk Van Gogh finger-painted the whole thing. I could feel my heart beating and blood flowing through my veins. It may have just been my imagination, but I only felt alive when I had dust. The air prickled my skin. It was like a vacation away from Pandemonium and, most importantly, myself.

I thought more clearly now, no burning hunger clouding my mind. That demon could be clear across the Broken Lands by now. Hell, he could have crossed the Bleeding Throat and been in Witch End. But no, he never would have gone there. Too many humans. He was still in the Broken Lands. I was sure of that.

What if I didn't find the little bugger? He'd totally blame me.

I stood up as the initial high faded and resolved into a warm feeling in my gut. I climbed a short rise and, when I reached the crest, there was the Really Big Pit of Fire. It had to be two miles long and just as wide. Flames reached two or three hundred feet in the air. On closer inspection, it wasn't one pit of fire but thousands of small fires. I could see gaps in the flames, small, narrow paths through the pit. I wasn't too happy about going through the blazes. I didn't know how good-looking I'd be as a skeleton. I'd probably have to take in my suit. But going around the fire would take too long and I wanted to get out of the Broken Lands as soon as possible.

I sucked in my gut and descended into the pit.

Damn it was hot in there, but it was a dry heat, so I wasn't complaining too much. The path zigged and zagged and widened a bit. I had to do a mambo to avoid the licking flames. I thought of going back. There was a good chance Oswald was already dead. Ah, who was I kidding? The little twerp is indestructible. He was probably sitting somewhere, tapping his foot, waiting for me to show up.

The flames crackled like thunder and zipped across the sky like lightning. Sweat dripped into my eyes, making it hard to see. A column of flame lashed out and nearly fried me, but I was able to jump out of the way. I wiped the sweat from my eyes and crept through the pit at a more careful pace.

I negotiated a difficult twist in the path and entered a clearing. I stood at the edge of a circle of white sand. A ten-foot-high wall of flame surrounded it. In the center sat a strange creature. He was an ugly sucker with a big, bulbous nose that hung past his bloated red lips. Instead of hair, tiny curls of flame danced atop his head. His dull, coal eyes watched me as I approached.

"Do you have blood for Ukobach?" he asked in a voice that crackled like a burning log. The fire demon held a poker with a glowing orange tip.

"I think I'll go with a no on that."

"I am Ukobach, the keeper of the infernal boilers. Appointed by Beelzebub himself."

"Dead Jack, Private Eye, here. Nice to meet your acquaintance, but you seem a long way from the infernal boilers."

"What have you heard?" His eyes darted from side to side.

"About...?"

"What have they been telling you about Ukobach?"

"They? They haven't been telling me anything about you. I've never heard of you."

The demon jumped up, flames shooting off him like a Roman candle. "Never *heard* of the great Ukobach!" he shouted. "The keeper of the infernal boilers!"

"Appointed by Beelzebub himself. Yeah, we went over that."

Ukobach pointed his poker to the sky and flames sprouted from the ground. One flaming column ignited right between my feet.

"On second thought, yeah, Ukobach. Is it Ukobach? I thought you said 'Yugo Block.' Everyone I know talks about Ukobach. They say he's a real hot head."

"Oh?" He looked as if he didn't know how to take that.

"In a good way."

"Do they fear me?"

"They're terrified. You should come to ShadowShade and give them a good scare."

"Ukobach cannot." The demon hung his head. "I have been banished from Hell, and tending to the pit is my punishment. Ukobach cannot leave."

"Out of curiosity, may I ask what you did to get banished from Hell? Seems a difficult thing to do."

"It happens more times than you'd think."

"Were you not infernal enough?"

His coal eyes burst into flames. "Ukobach is as infernal as any Prince of Hell! He is their equal! Nay, he is their better!"

"You were probably *too* infernal. I can tell. I'm sure they were jealous."

"You are more correct than you know."

"Well, it was nice chatting with you, but I need to be moseying along." When I tried to pass the fiery fellow, he said, "You may not leave without permission from the keeper of the infernal boilers."

"I thought we went over that. You're no longer the keeper of the infernal boilers."

"You will have safe passage through the pit—"

"Okay, that's very kind of you," I said and once again tried to get past Ukobach. He blocked me with his poker.

"—after you give Ukobach your blood."

"You need just a sample or something?"

"Ukobach will need all of it."

"If you haven't noticed, I'm a zombie. I don't have such great blood."

"Your blood is exactly what Ukobach needs."

"And what do you need it for?"

"To make the oil that fuels the infernal boilers, Ukobach needs the blood of the damned."

"Now wait a minute. I'm far from damned."

Ukobach grinned and tiny sparks danced at the corners of his mouth. "You are a member of the soulless. You are beyond damned."

"I don't know who *you've* been talking to, but this whole soulless thing has gotten really overblown. I do fine without a soul."

"You are a marked man. Damned for eternity. When the soulless die the absolute death, they are sent to a very special place in the deepest, darkest depths of Hell. Pandemonium will seem a paradise."

"You make a great pitch, but I think I'm going to keep my blood."

Ukobach held up his poker, which now glowed white hot.

"When Ukobach has collected enough, Ukobach will be welcomed back to Hell. Beelzebub promised Ukobach himself."

The joke was on him. There was no way out of Pandemonium. You'd think demons were smart enough not to believe a Prince of Hell.

"This place isn't hot enough for you?" I asked. "You want to go back to Hell?"

"Ukobach does not request your blood."

This Ukobach didn't strike me as a particularly smart demon. He must have been of an inferior order. I played along. "You know what? You look like you deserve a break from this place.

So, I'm going to contribute to the Get Ukobach Back to Hell Fund. You can have all the blood you need. Should I just split open a vein?"

Ukobach look confused. He probably never had anyone volunteer before. After a few moments of silence, he said, "You have chosen wisely, damned one. Ukobach is strong. He is not to be trifled with. There is no need for you to cut yourself. Ukobach will roast you over a vat into which the blood will collect."

"Where's this vat?"

"Ukobach has to get it."

"Go right ahead. Is it close?"

Ukobach looked around like it might have been sitting right next to him the whole time.

"Wait here," he said and took off. He slipped through the wall of fire and disappeared. This guy was a total moron.

I didn't waste any time. I headed to the far end of the fire wall and stopped. There didn't seem to be any opening. I could risk it and jump through. Maybe it was only a few inches thick. Or I could cremate myself.

Then I had a brilliant idea. (Perhaps there was a brain in my skull after all.) I unbuckled my belt and held it with the buckle at the bottom end. Then I began to whip the belt in a circle, creating a giant fan. When I worked up enough power, I brought it closer to the fire wall. Just as I had hoped, the flames parted. I still couldn't see beyond the fire wall, so I whipped the belt harder and entered when I had created a nice-sized hole.

Whoosh, whoosh, whoosh. The flames spread and I stepped through the tunnel I had created. The wall was pretty thick. I never would have made it had I tried running through. I trudged through the tunnel for several seconds and I still hadn't come to the end. My arm began to tire and the belt fan slowed. The tunnel constricted. I hurried on. The flames danced just centimeters from the top of my fedora and I sunk down. Though my arm felt close to giving out, I whipped that belt like I was whipping a rented pegasus. Then I saw a break in the wall.

"Ukobach needs your blood!" the demon yelled.

I didn't have much more strength in my arm. The flames closed in on me and I dove.

I hit the sand and felt my right foot go up in flames. I stood and tried to stamp it out, but that just made the flames creep up my leg. Crap! I filled my hat with the white sand and poured it on my burning limb. It took three attempts to extinguish the fire. Now I was going to need new shoes and pants. This case was costing me an entire wardrobe.

Ukobach slipped out of the fire wall, his poker raised high.

"Ukobach is strong," he said. "He is not to be trifled with."

"Trifle with this," I said, after refilling my hat with sand. I reared back and threw it at the fire demon. The sand hit him smack dab in the face. The little flame curls around his head went out.

"Ukobach's hair!" he screamed. "Ukobach's beautiful fire curls!"

He dropped the poker and patted his head. He ran around in a circle, screaming, "Ukobach is bald! Ukobach is bald! Ukobach is bald!"

Jeez, this guy was vain.

I grabbed the poker and power-shambled out of there.

"Ukobach cannot return to Hell like this!" I heard the demon shouting as I dashed around columns of flame. I soon discovered that, if I waved the poker, the flames moved. Like an orchestra conductor I whipped that poker through the air, conducting the flames away from me. It was smooth sailing until Ukobach regained his senses and came after me.

"You bastard! You thief! Come back with my poker!"

Though pokerless, Ukobach wasn't without power.

The flames grew brighter and more violent. Even with the poker, I was having a difficult time moving them out of my way. Flames shot at me from all sides. But never mind the flames, it was stifling hot. It was like being in the middle of the sun. Zombie sweat, the worst kind of sweat, covered me.

As I ran up the lip of the pit, a dragon made of flames came screeching toward me. It belched a mouthful of fire at me. I waved the poker at the streaking column of flames and they vanished along with the dragon.

Fire erupted from the ground, but through it I could see the edge of the pit just twenty feet above me. I rushed toward it, slashing the flames with the poker.

"Thief! Give Ukobach back his poker!"

He was right behind me. I turned to stick him with his poker, but it turned scorching hot and I dropped it. Ukobach laughed and picked up his instrument.

I made a mad dash up the pit wall. Just feet from the top, my legs gave out. I tried crawling, but flames of rope wrapped around my ankles and dragged me down.

Ukobach drew intricate patterns in the air with the poker, like a madman writing in his diary. He really was much uglier without the flaming hair. Maybe he could hide it with a hat or something.

I'm still unsure of what happened next. There was a flutter and a growl and a screech. Then I was being pulled out of the pit. Arms wrapped around my chest. I looked down. They were hairy, muscular arms. They were the most beautiful arms I had ever seen.

Ukobach sent up a wall of flame, but whoever dragged me away didn't hesitate. My rescuer tossed us both through the flames and we tumbled onto the ground outside the Really Big Pit of Fire.

Ukobach stood at the edge with his poker, jabbing it in my direction.

"You really are trapped here, aren't you?" I said after I stood.

Ukobach sniffed and snorted fire and made an obscene gesture with his poker.

I patted out the burning parts of my suit and came face to face with the Good Samaritan. Amazingly, he was uglier than Ukobach.

8

LIKE A BAT OUT OF HELL

As I approached, the bat man cowered.

"Thanks for saving my life." I extended my hand. The creature stepped back, eyeing me warily. "You did save my life, right? I mean you didn't pull me out of the pit just to eat me?"

He crouched and froze in place. The giant bat had a hunched back and apparently took baths in fire pits. Burn marks—angry red, raised scars—covered his face and body. Most of his fur was missing, with just a patch or three erupting randomly from his haunches and chest. The creature's wing membranes were missing, too, though the bone structure remained. Perhaps Ukobach burned them off. The bat's misshapen and bent form looked as if someone had taken it apart and rearranged it as a joke.

The demon licked his bumpy, blistered lips.

"So...are you from around here?" I asked.

He bared bloodstained fangs.

Just then, perhaps to break up the tension, the creature snatched up a purple lizard as it scampered by. He slit its throat with his teeth and lapped up the blood with a thick, flickering tongue. Great! My rescuer was a vampire, too.

I gave no indication I was hungry for purple lizard, but the bat man said, "It's mine!" He held the dripping lizard against his chest. "Mine!" he repeated and crammed what was left of the little bugger into his mouth. Purple blood oozed down the bat's chin.

"I must keep what is mine," he said, then belched. A stench worse than a ghoul's armpit after a ten-mile jog hit me head-on. I nearly gagged.

"I wish I could repay you for saving me from the pit. I hope my thanks is enough."

"You can repay me with dust, zombie." I didn't like the way he said *zombie*. It felt as though he had a problem with my kind, but then I saw the hunger in his eyes. Another fookin dust-head.

"Give me your address. I'll send you some if I ever get my hands on the stuff." He stuck his big, ugly head up to my chest and gave a sniff, his melted nostrils twitching like a demonic rabbit.

"I can smell it," he said.

"That's not dust, pally. Must have been something I had for lunch."

"I know fairy dust when I smell it." The vampire bat stared into my eyes.

"Look, I need that dust. It's medicinal. Without it, I'll eat half of Pandemonium. I'd love to help you, but it's a life and death situation."

The bat shot out a clawed hand and, before I could blink, he was holding up a baggie of dust.

"Hey!"

The bat laughed.

"Not nice, boyo. Give it back."

He held up the dust, and when I tried to grab it, he snatched it away.

"I am Camazotz the Thief. You cannot steal from me."

The creature glared at me like he had nothing to lose and I knew messing with him would be a mistake. "Listen, bats, keep it. Consider it payment in full. Now I'll be going, okay? I have some saving to do myself. Fifty-two cats, to be exact."

The bat's giddiness evaporated. He returned to his cowering bit and backed away from me. "Cats?" he asked.

"Know anything about them? The goblins' missing cats?"

The bat shook his head. I wasn't convinced.

"Camazotz the Thief, huh? Steal any cats lately?"

"No!" He spit on the ground. "Camazotz would never steal a cat!"

"A thief with morals. I admire that. You must know other infernal thieves, though. Maybe there's someone you know who likes kitty cats? Someone with a whisker fetish?"

Zotzy kept shaking his head, like he was a real dunzy. He wouldn't give up anything. Honor among thieves, I guess.

"Maybe more dust will refresh your memory," I said and forked over another baggie of the stuff. I nearly yanked it back, but the bat snatched it up. His eyes lit up like the worst addicts from ShadowShade's dust dens.

"Give me more!" he demanded.

"When you give me the info, and only if it's legit. This is the best batch of Special D you'll ever come across, Zotzy. Real killer-diller. Believe me."

I could see the bat's heart throbbing in his chest.

"Another baggie and I'll show you," Zotzy said.

"Half a bag and you'll get it when we get there."

The bat man thought a moment, and then nodded.

"Very well."

The burned demon didn't budge, though. "First we must cross over Corpse Hill," he said.

"I'm great with corpses. They're my people."

"It's a haunted place." The demon looked spooked.

"I wouldn't want it any other way. Where do we go once we're past Corpse Hill?"

"To the Broken Palace and the Duke."

"The Duke?"

"The cats are in his possession."

"Lead the way, Bats."

Camazotz lurched forward, like a hunchback with two broken legs and arthritis. It was going to be a long walk.

"Ukobach cannot wait till you're burning in the depths of Hell for eternity, you soulless sack of shit!" Ukobach shouted from the edge of the Really Big Pit of Fire. I had completely forgotten the little mother-sparker. "You are damned! Ratzinger is coming for you! Then you will know hell!"

Ratzinger. I hadn't heard that name spoken aloud in decades. A ball of heat shot up my spine. I thought I was on fire again, but then I realized it was just my imagination.

"What do you know about—?" I tried to utter the psycho's name, but it wouldn't move past my lips. Ukobach laughed like a horror show bad guy.

"Let's blow," I said to Camazotz, and we left.

Ukobach's maniacal laughter followed us long after we left the pit behind.

9

I FOUND MY THRILL
ON CORPSE HILL

I **tried striking up a conversation with Zotzy as we** sauntered to Corpse Hill. He wasn't much of a conversationalist.

"So a giant bat, huh? What's that like? Are there many of you?"

"I am one of a kind."

"Yeah, me too. Well, one of a few. I've never seen a giant bat before."

"I just said I was one of a kind."

"So, no giant bat mom or dad?"

"I am Camazotz."

"Right. Okay. Mystery solved."

"I am a god."

That explained a lot. "Pandemonium's not too kind to gods, is it? No worshipers here."

"I was feared and loved. They gave me their blood."

"I feel for you, pally. I really do."

We trudged across the battered ground. The stench of brimstone and rot wafted up from the fissures. I took out a hellfire stick. They had all dried. That was one good thing about going through the Really Big Pit of Fire. I lit it and Camazotz went nuts. I held up the lighter and the bat god shrunk in terror.

"This? The lighter? You're afraid of the fire?"

The bat god gave a tiny nod.

"What the hell happened to you?" I asked. "Did Ukobach do that to you?" I gestured to his burned-up body. "Did he set you on fire?"

The bat god shook his head. I put away the lighter and the Lucky Dragon.

"If you don't mind me asking, how did you end up like this?"

Camazotz shook his head again. I let it go, and we continued on.

I didn't trust this bat god. First of all, gods have huge egos. They're only out for themselves, and this one was broken and abandoned, not to mention a sassy little dust thief. I was dumb, but I wasn't stupid. This whole thing could be a set-up.

"If you're so afraid of fire, why did you pull me out of the pit?" I asked.

"I saved you for the dust."

"Good old dust. It's saved my rotten arse many times before."

We strolled in awkward silence until we reached the foot of Corpse Hill. Camazotz stopped and glared up the steep, zigzagging path.

"The Duke is just over the hill," he said and turned to leave.

"Whoa, batzy! We had a deal."

"You don't need me to take you over the hill, coward."

"And the name-calling! What about the dust? You don't guide me all the way, you get no dust. And I can see that you need it. In fact, I've never seen anyone need it as bad as you, buddy."

"The place is haunted. Bad spirits." The palooka trembled.

He flashed out a bat hand, but I was ready for him. I took a step back and to the side.

"You're not stealing any more dust from me, batty. You'll have to earn it."

I patted him on his back. "You're in good hands," I said. "Corpses are my people."

Camazotz inhaled and we headed up the hill.

Corpse Hill was the perfect name for the place. Bodies seemed to grow out of the ground like daisies. Some were propped up against trees looking like drunks sleeping off a bender. Others were face down in the dirt. Most of them were demons or ogres or goblins, but I spotted quite a few human witches and warlocks, too. Many of the bodies were incomplete, missing an arm or leg or bottom half. I wondered if that's how they died or if the amputations happened postmortem.

Unlike the plains of the Broken Lands, here there were plenty of trees. Well, tree trunks anyway. Dead, twisted things that rose out of the ground like reaching hands.

As you would expect among corpses, the hill was silent. (Notice I didn't say "silent as a grave." That would have been too corny.) Sickly, pink-lined clouds scudded overhead as a warm wind began to blow.

Camazotz's naked wing bones vibrated and he stiffened.

"I feel right at home," I said, trying to calm him. "I may even retire out here one day. Dead people are harmless. It's the living ones you have to watch out for."

The tree trunks thinned out. Up ahead, to my right, I spotted an area lost in shadows. Camazotz saw it, too, I noticed. His wings twittered a bit more, and he quickened his step, which I could tell was a real chore for him.

"Let's hurry," he said. "Stay on this side of the path."

He tried to pull me to left. It was obvious he didn't want me to see what was up ahead. I pulled away from the bat god and hustled up the path ahead of him.

The shadowy area was wide and a few yards off the path, on a slight decline. No trees stood here. I stepped off the path and looked down.

It wasn't a shadow. It was a grave. A mass grave.

From the looks of it, the hole was hastily dug and not too deep. But it didn't need to be, because it was full of little folk. Fairies of all sorts—pixies, sprites, elves, gnomes, brownies. Interestingly, there were no leprechauns.

Their bodies were thrown in the pit willy-nilly. Body on top of body. Even in the dark, I could see they had been mutilated and done so deliberately. One pixie had its wings pulled off and shoved into its mouth. Another's head was split in half. The elves had their ears cut off.

Fairies usually stick to their home turf in the Red Garden. A few venture out to ShadowShade, but never to the Broken Lands.

Camazotz grabbed me by the shoulders. "We have to go," he said.

"What happened here?"

The bat god shook his head in disgust. "The Duke," he said. "He's a madman. Please, we must go."

"He killed all of those fairies? Why the hell would he do that?"

"I said we need to leave!" he shouted, and the scars on his face grew redder.

"You're keeping something from me." The bat god backed away, shaking his head in shame. "If you won't tell me, I'll have *them* tell me."

I dove into the fairy grave. Camazotz gave a tiny cry and then I heard his hurried footsteps as he took off back the way we had come. I was on my own now.

I was instantly surprised by the lack of a stench. Fairy corpses smelled sweet, like lilacs and grass. I wish I knew their secret. I searched for a fairy that wasn't in terrible condition. It was hard work. The Duke had really gone to town on these poor bastards. I grabbed a kobold. He was naked, but other than a nearly severed head, he seemed in good shape. I pulled out some fairy dust. I dipped my finger into the baggie and rubbed the dust on the kobold's lips and tongue.

I cradled the poor thing's body in my arms. He looked more like a human child than a fairy. But the pointy ears, odd-shaped eyes, and otherworldly beauty gave him away.

He projectile-vomited blood onto my chest. That ruined the illusion a bit. When he was done bleeding all over me, he looked up and smiled.

"We don't have much time," I said. "Tell me what happened to you and your friends."

His face twisted in agony and terror. "The bald one," he croaked out. Blood bubbled up in his cut throat.

"Ukobach?" I said and then I remembered that his baldness was relatively new. "The bald one killed you? Do you mean the Duke?"

The kobold's eyes glazed over. He seemed to be looking within. "He destroy all," he said. "Stole Jupiter Stone."

A Jupiter Stone? They were the most powerful and dangerous objects in Pandemonium. The Cyclops on Monster Island supposedly made them from a thunderbolt thrown by Zeus. There had been four, but they were all thought to have been lost or destroyed at the end of the Great Fairy War.

"What about the cats?" I asked. "What do you know about the cats?"

"The interdimensional ones hurt."

"What are you talking about? I think I gave you too much dust."

"The thief stole the Jupiter Stone. To destroy all."

"Camazotz?"

"What are you saying? Camazotz stole the Jupiter Stone? I don't understand." Maybe this kobold was in worse condition than I had thought. He wasn't making much sense.

The blood from the kobold's neck had turned thick and black. He gurgled and went slack. A voice came through the kobold's mouth. It wasn't his. "Don't talk to the dead, Jack," it said. "You should know better than anyone else how duplicitous they are."

It had been so long since I heard that voice in anything but my dreams that I needed a moment to place it. When I did, I swear my skin prickled.

"Ratzinger?" I whispered. I shook the corpse. "Is that you, Ratzinger, you Nazi scum?" I screamed, but all I heard was the wind rushing over Corpse Hill.

I climbed out of the grave. (How fookin cliché.)

When I returned to the path, I checked the dust in my pockets. Yep, half of it was gone. I made my way up the hill, kicking myself for trusting a guy whose last name was "The Thief." Now I knew why he was so nervous about crossing over the hill. He didn't want me to discover the mass grave. He may have stolen a Jupiter Stone. Did he maybe kill those fairies, too?

I didn't have time to think about it. Not all the corpses on Corpse Hill were dead. When I got to the summit, I was greeted by the welcoming committee.

A more ragtag group of ghouls and skeletons I had never seen before. The ghouls were covered in mud and dried blood and ash. Their clothes, if they were wearing any, were in tatters. The skeletons were in worse shape. With all the cracks and splinters in their bones, it was amazing they were able to stand.

Reanimated corpses slunk out of the shadows and from under the ground and behind tree stumps. They surrounded me.

"Hey, fellas," I said. "Who died and left you in charge?"

No one laughed. Apparently, their senses of humor hadn't been reanimated along with their bodies. The undead closed in. I could see the hunger in their eyes. Well, at least the ones who had eyes.

I didn't want to pull the "do you know who I am?" card, mostly because it's never worked before, but I am persistent.

"Gentlemen," I said, "some professional courtesy here. From one ghoul to another. I don't know if you know this, but I'm *the* Dead Jack, Pandemonium's famed private investigator." They stopped in their tracks.

One of the ghouls stepped forward. His right eye hung down to his cheek from its stalk. He wore what might have been a suit once, but was now just a tie, a sleeve, and one pant leg. "Dead Jack?" he asked in a raspy voice.

"In the rotten flesh." I flashed him a smile. He didn't smile back. Then I noticed he had no lower jaw.

"Never heard of you."

"What's your name?"

"Bloodletter."

"Is that German?"

The ghoul made a move. I sidestepped and threw a right cross. It connected with the side of his skull. His dangling eye popped off and rolled down the hill. Bloodletter took off after it.

Another ghoul stepped up. I really wasn't in the mood to fight these idiots.

"Hey, listen," I said. "I—"

The ghoul said, "Dead Jack! I know you. I once saw you eat a three-headed dog in under ten minutes."

"Or it wouldn't have been free," I said. Seems my reputation did precede me.

"Didn't you recover *The Book of the Three Towers* from Mordread?" a corpse with no legs or arms asked.

"I nearly took the big dirt nap with that one."

The ghouls clamored and rushed toward me. I'm sure it was rare for a true-life celebrity to be in their midst. If only Oswald could have seen this.

"Yeah, the Dead Dick," a tall skeleton with a top hat said. "Didn't you go wild a few years back and eat a bunch of innocent fairies?"

Quiet returned to Corpse Hill. The dead watched me with questioning eyes. I grinned. They didn't grin back. "Is anyone in Pandemonium really innocent?" I blurted out. "I'm sure you'd do the same given the chance."

"How did they taste?" a ghoul asked. "Are they as chewy as they say?"

I laughed nervously. The creeps wanted the gory details. But I didn't remember much about the incident. I only recalled Oswald making me swear to stop the zombie feasts afterward, an oath I've mostly kept since. "Fellas," I said, "I'd love to sit here all night and talk with you about my exploits—some of which have been greatly exaggerated—but I need to get to the Broken Palace."

The ghouls exchanged glances with one another.

"Stay away from there," said the skeleton with the top hat. "Bad news."

"No choice," I said. "The Duke has my friend—I mean my associate—and I need to rescue some cats."

"We'd go with you," the torso said, "but we don't want to."

"No worries, guys. If you could just point me in the direction of the palace."

"Just follow this path north. You can't miss it."

As I descended the hill, the undead tagged along, like lost puppies, asking me annoying questions.

"Jack, is it true a homunculus was living inside your skull?"

"Jack, what does troll taste like?"

"How do you keep your suit so clean?"

At the bottom of the hill, the dead bunch refused to go any farther. I passed out business cards, shook hands, signed a couple of skulls, and took my leave. Like I said, corpses are my people.

10

THEY BUILT THIS CITY
ON ROCK AND BONES

After a mile-long trek through desolate terrain, I came upon the Broken City.

As ruined cities went, this one was apocalyptic. It was straight out of Revelations. Black smoke darkened the already dark sky and fires that gave off no heat rose from the ground. Temples of obsidian and mansions of bone lay in ruins. Skulls and carcasses filled the streets, which were stained with ancient blood. The only thing missing was the Whore of Babylon, and I was sure if I looked hard enough I'd find her.

I entered the city.

I made my way down a wide boulevard, stepping over bones and debris. The smell of sulfur and burning and blood grew stronger as I moved deeper into the city.

Shadows moved among the ruins. The spirits whispered on the wind and what they had to say wasn't worth listening to. I moved faster.

It looked as if a great battle had been fought here. I hadn't heard about it, but not much that goes on in the Broken Lands makes the news.

I climbed a heap of skulls and, when I reached the summit, I spotted the palace. It resembled a bat with the main building as the head and the two annexes as the wings. The place was a hundred yards wide and half as tall. It was all bone columns and ramparts covered in shadows. Huge red eyes glowed from between the columns and stared out at the night. Most of the palace still stood, but huge areas were caved in or obliterated. A moat of fire surrounded the whole kit and caboodle.

Between me and the palace was about two hundred yards of hellish landscape. Large pieces of earth, like shards of glass, jutted into the air, and fire or lava filled all the fissures. It looked like a Titan had smashed the ground to pieces in a fit of rage.

I slipped as I descended the pile of skulls and tumbled onto the fiery plain. I stood, dusted myself off, and fixed my hat. I didn't know if those red eyes could see me, but I decided it was a good idea to hide. I slipped behind a basilisk skeleton and watched the palace.

Demons kept patrol on the ramparts, which were dotted with torches, and they flew in and out of the eastern wing of the compound.

The place was a damn fortress. How the blazes was I going to get in there? Brainstorm? I didn't even know what that meant.

I lit my second-to-last hellfire stick, took a deep drag. Only one thought came to me: Knock on the front door. Simple. Easy. No muss, no fuss. Oswald, no doubt, would want to tunnel under the palace or parachute onto the roof or pole-vault over the ramparts. The little man had some big balls. But why bother with such complicated plans? Complicated plans always fall apart. The easiest solution was always the best solution. Someone smart once said that, I think.

I hop-scotched from one piece of broken earth to another. I nearly lost my balance halfway there and went tumbling into a pit of fire. The closer I got to the palace the colder it got, despite all the fires.

I made it to the moat with only a few dozen more burns to my suit.

There was a drawbridge, which of course was pulled up.

I noticed a few demons looking down at me from the ramparts and their eyes burned like the black fires of damnation.

"A little help for a zombie in distress?" I shouted and pointed at the drawbridge. A moment or two passed and the drawbridge came creaking down. I congratulated myself, but then I figured they probably needed to add a little flavor to their soup.

I crossed the bridge. The stench of that moat was worse than Cerberus's breath after dinner.

When I reached the palace's twin doors, which were just shorter than an ice giant and about the width of a sphinx, I gave them a hard rap. They felt as if they were made of human skin.

Eventually, the doors screeched open and thick, oily shadows spilled out of the palace. A demon doorman appeared, a black creature framed against the blacker interior of the palace. He opened his gigantic mouth, showing me his sharp, wet teeth. He took a step forward, his nostrils twitching. He sniffed me up and down.

"Zombie," he said.

"I'm in a bit of a pickle. My rental pegasus broke down up the road. Do you have a phone I can use?"

The demon picked its long teeth.

"A telegraph?" I asked.

The demon drooled.

"A carrier gremlin? I'd like to call a miracle-worker."

"Zombie," the demon said with fat ropes of saliva running down its muzzle.

It was obvious what the creature was after. "Look, I taste worse than kraken sushi left out on a hot Pandemonium night."

"I've had worse."

"Really? Have you ever eaten three-day-old bladderpig?"

"Four-day old."

"Spoiled sea hag?"

"Twice. Have you ever eaten petrified troll?"

"Come on, of course. But if you want a treat, try leprechaun. So sweet and juicy."

"I've heard that."

"Let me use the phone and I'll tell you where you can pick some up."

I didn't wait for an invitation. I stepped inside. A huge portrait beside two torches dominated the grand foyer. Several other, smaller portraits and a couple of statues depicted the same man: a tall, gaunt fellow with intense black eyes, a red goatee, and a bald head. It took a moment for me to place that face. I last saw it twenty-five years ago in a dust den in ShadowShade.

"Is that the Duke of Pandemonium?" I asked, pretty sure it was. "Does he live here?" I tried to put a squeal in my voice. I think I succeeded.

The demon bowed his head. "Of course. He is our master."

"Me and the Duke go way back. We used to party in Shadow-Shade years ago. I used to hook him up with dust." The demon didn't seem impressed. "Tell your master his old pal Dead Jack is here."

The demon seemed doubtful, but he nodded and slipped into the shadows. I heard the *whoosh* of demon wings in the depths of the palace and shrieks, of pain or joy, I wasn't sure, and it probably didn't matter here. Demonic laughter rolled through the long halls. If I had any hair left on my body, it would have been standing up.

A few minutes later, the demon returned.

"Come," he said.

He led me into the palace. It smelled much worse inside than outside. The air reeked of brimstone and blood and rot and turned earth. We passed the ballroom. Inside, vampires feasted on a group of what looked like tentacled squid men. They didn't look up.

Demons and orcs and gargoyles passed us in the halls. Some gave me dirty looks. Pieces of the ceiling showered down like confetti at a ticker-tape parade.

"Can I smoke in here?" I asked, mostly as a joke. There didn't seem to be anything you couldn't do here.

The demon didn't respond, so I lit up a hellfire stick. I took a couple of puffs before the demon snatched it out of my mouth. He didn't say why. It was my last one.

He stopped before a black door and opened it.

"Wait inside," he said.

"Am I ever going to get out of this room?" The demon didn't answer.

I poked my head in and did a quick scan. It was a large hall. The right wall had crumbled to dust and most of the ceiling had collapsed. Moonlight drifted in and covered everything in a red tint. At the end of the room, an obsidian throne sat on a dais. No one was inside.

I stepped in.

The door immediately slammed behind me. I was about to check if it was locked, but I was accosted by a swarm of demonic flies. The little buggers buzzed around my head, chatting about me as if I weren't there.

"Oh, a corpse!"

"Good eating they are."

"Perfect for nesting."

"I see a perfect spot to lay eggs."

"I can hear you," I said.

"Did you hear that?" one of them said.

"The corpse is speaking!"

"I didn't hear it. What did it say?"

"It's just your imagination, Carl."

"He doesn't look too bright."

"Stupid-looking thing, isn't he?"

"Maybe he's not worth infesting."

"We may catch something, you know?"

"Bug off!" I shouted as I swatted at the infernal insects.

They dodged my hand and returned to circling. Little fat horns jutted out of their heads and tiny spikes protruded from their legs.

"Is that an insult?" one of them said.

"Told us to bug off, did he?"

"A pun! The corpse is using puns? How utterly sad."

"His jokes are as dead as he is."

"He should crawl back into the grave from which he escaped."

One of the flies bit me on the cheek. I smacked him with the back of my hand. He dropped straight to the ground. Gave a *bzzt-bzzt* and died.

"The corpse killed Carl!"

"Scram!" I shouted and poked at them with my lit lighter. They got the message and flew off.

Feet thumped. The ground shook. Something huge and most likely dangerous approached. I cracked my knuckles and got into a fighting stance.

From the other end of the hall, a horde of demons appeared. Slimy, scaly suckers with big, misshapen heads and slavering muzzles flooded the hall, one troop from the left and another from the right. Like automatons, they lined up in perfect, tight rows before the dais and paid me no mind. I remained in position, ready for whatever.

The hall got a bit stuffy and smelled something awful. I could feel heat coming off the demons. It was the only heat in the cold, cold room.

Music began to play. First a solitary drum, and then an orchestra, full of brass instruments and atonal clanging.

A spotlight hit the throne from directly above.

A public address system screeched to life and crackled, before a deep, guttural voice said:

"Chattel and chums...put your claws together for the Lord of the Broken!" The demons drove their clawed feet into the ground and clapped their taloned hands. Their wings snapped. The voice continued: "The Baron of the Banished! The Ruler of the Wastelands and Beyond! The Redeemer, that Big, Big Dreamer. Our Master of Disaster. The one, the only...Duke of Pandemonium!"

The room filled with a dark electricity. The clamor was deafening. The heat got so intense I thought the place was about to burst into flames.

A figure in black descended from the shadows above. He waved to the hordes and blew kisses as he floated down. I thought I saw a wire. The Duke dropped onto the throne.

"Hey," he said in an apathetic way and rested his head on his left fist. "Where's our esteemed guest? Get him up here."

The demons turned to me. I didn't move. One of them grabbed me, picked me up, and passed me to another creature. They kept passing me up along until I was standing before the throne.

I instantly recognized my old friend. But back then his name was Eddie McCrawley. He was one of the only humans I had ever palled around with. He was a wild man, one of the biggest dust-heads I had ever known. He could snort an entire kilo in one night, and he often did.

He hadn't changed much, except for the lack of hair. Tall and pale, black eyes like obsidian mirrors. A perpetual wicked grin. He was always the showman, but never anything like this.

"A fookin zombie!" he shouted. "You guys didn't tell me it was a damn brain-licker! I thought it was someone *alive*! Someone *important*!"

Eddie jumped up, his eyes wide in disbelief. It had been a while since we hung out. Maybe he had forgotten about me.

"Someone eat this guy and stop wasting my time."

A demon grabbed me from behind. The Duke turned and began to walk away. I was surprised he didn't float back up through the ceiling.

"Eddie!" I shouted. "It's me, Jack!"

He turned and the long tails of his high-collared tunic swished. "Never heard of any Eddie and I sure as fook don't know any bag of bones named Zach."

"No, *Jack*! Dead Jack! We used to hang out at the dust den in Little Valhalla."

"Sorry. Doesn't ring a bell. Eat him and grind up the bones for the hellhounds."

The demon's talons dug into my shoulders. I closed my eyes, waiting for the drop. The Duke howled in laughter. I opened my eyes and he stood before me. He was shaking his head, a big smirk on his face.

"You dirty, rotten corpse! You always fell for my practical jokes!"

I tried to hide my shakes. "You haven't changed, Eddie," I said.

"My name has changed." His smiled evaporated. "I go by the Duke now. And I'm no longer a two-bit hustler. All of these infernal creatures are my loyal subjects."

"Too modest for the King or the Lord of Pandemonium, huh?"

"I gave it serious thought. But I was always a fan of the Duke, John Wayne. And the Duke of Pandemonium just sounds so nifty, doesn't it? What brings you to our part of hell, Jack? Working on one of your little cases?"

"Me? No. I'm retired."

"When did that happen?"

"About two hellfire sticks ago."

He laughed, but I wasn't sure if it was at me or with me. "You're far from ShadowShade, friend."

"I'm on vacation. Seeing the sights. And wouldn't you know it, my pegasus rental breaks down and dies? Do you have a phone I can use?"

"A phone?"

"Yeah, you know that thing you speak into and people far away can hear you?"

"Sorry, Jack. We keep things pretty simple around here."

"You and all your demon friends?"

"I always kept interesting company, didn't I?" He slapped me on the back, hard. I stumbled a step or two forward.

Despite the weird theatrics and the demon army, I was having a hard time believing my old pal was responsible for killing all those fairies up on Corpse Hill. Then a demon fell out of formation. Just a step. But enough to make a sound.

The Duke turned. "Who moved?" he said. "Who the *fook* moved?"

The demons didn't say a word. The Duke walked up and down the line like a military general, eyeing each infernal creature. "Is this a fookin *carnival* show? Have I not *prepared* you? There must be no *weak* links for what is to come!"

The demon must have gotten nervous because he slipped again and the Duke spotted it. He snapped his fingers and the other demons descended on their colleague, pulling off his wings and arms and legs.

The Duke returned to me, smirked like a man who's just been fitted with a straitjacket, and said, as if nothing had happened: "To be honest, I'm glad you're here, Jack. I miss the old days. Why don't you stick around? We can reminisce. We're about to have dinner."

"I already ate today." I watched as the demon's horns were wrenched off his head.

"I hope it wasn't anyone I know." He laughed and gave me another chummy slap on the back.

Actually, it probably was someone he knew. "I can't make any promises," I said and giggled nervously.

"Forget food then. Have a drink with us."

"Do you have any Devil Boy?"

"I'm sure I can procure some." He winked. "You caught me at a bad time, Jack. Things are extremely busy around here. In fact, I have some urgent matters to attend to."

He probably had some demonic fly wings to pull off.

"Jevex," he said, "give Jack a tour of the palace." And with that, he left.

Jevex—he was the demon who opened the palace door—stepped forward and said, "Follow me."

As I followed Jevex, the errant demon's head was torn from his body and passed around the room like a trophy. It was going to be an interesting dinner.

11

DINNER FOR DEMONS (AND ASSORTED OTHER MONSTERS)

The tour was brief.

Jevex showed me the ruined gardens, which were nothing but clods of dirt full of bones; the ruined chapel, where the inverted crosses were right-side up; and the hall of mirrors, which was actually a hall of shattered glass. When we reached a wooden door covered in Enochian script, Jevex said, "It's time for dinner." And then he did an about-face.

"What's beyond that door?" I asked.

"That's the Duke's chambers."

And why did the Duke need to protect his chambers with a secret angelic language? Maybe he was afraid of his minions busting in and tearing his head off.

The last stop on the tour was the dining room.

Like the rest of the palace, it was a wreck. Holes filled the ceiling and the walls. The back wall was completely gone. The remaining walls were charred from what must have been a huge fire that swept through the room.

Guests sat around the thirty-yard-long dining table, digging into their stomach-churning meals. They put me a few seats from the head of the table. I was surrounded by Pandemonium's biggest scum—ogres, vampires, trolls, lizard men, demons of all sorts. And people were disgusted when they saw me eat? I was a dainty little eater compared to these hungry hellions. The ogre beside me slopped up a dark brown soup that seemed to be made of human bones and maggots. I think I spotted a mole-man eating a deep-fried rat on an obsidian plate at the end of the table. Fortunately, cat wasn't on the menu, or Oswald.

An ancient-looking vampire sat across from me. "I have been told you are an intelligent corpse," he said. His mustard-colored fangs dripped with blood from his sanguine milkshake.

"I'm a zombie genius actually," I said. "The only member of the revenant branch of Mensa."

"More like a smart-ass zombie, if you ask me," said a woman with the head of an alligator and the claws of a hawk. She bit the head off a live chicken and drank its blood.

If I had an appetite, I would have lost it.

I recognized one of the guests: Madgogg. I was once hired to rescue a pixie from the ogre's Upper West Side lair. He flared his nostrils at me. I ignored him and drank my Devil Boy. Eddie had plenty, and I planned on drinking as much as my innards would hold. I was already on my third glass. Eddie hadn't joined our little soirée yet. I presumed he wanted to be fashionably late.

"I also understand you are a detective," the vampire said. He took another long, disgusting slurp of his blood shake. I had to turn away.

This bloodsucker sure was curious. "Some people call me a dead dick," I said, "but I don't like those people."

The vamp snorted and I swear some of that frothy blood came out of his nose. I *had* to try to make him laugh again.

"Do you have a...?" He raised an eyebrow and nodded down at my nether regions.

I caught his drift. It wasn't the first time I was asked if my man parts had been resurrected, too. "Let's say I'm undead, but I'm not completely undead." I winked.

The joke bombed. No frothy blood out of the nose this time, just a smirk.

"That's all that matters," he said. "If I couldn't get it up after all these centuries, I'd put a stake through my own heart."

"Isn't the whole vampire thing sexual? All that blood sucking is just a metaphor, right?"

"There's a sexual component, yes, but sometimes it's just about the blood." He ran a long, bony finger around the rim of his glass, catching blood milkshake residue. Then he put it to his lips and gave it a good suck. He was giving me quite a show.

"Is there a lot of sex going on in the palace?" I asked. "Is this the preparation for a big monster orgy?"

The vamp chortled but again no nose blood. I was beginning to feel like a failure.

"If things go right, we're going to have the biggest monster orgy in the history of existence."

"Yeah? If what goes right?"

The vampire gave me an expression that said "you don't know?" But before he could fill me in, the Duke made his grand entrance.

He swept into the room like he owned the place. Actually, he probably did. He sat at the head of the table. A bullheaded demon sat to his left. Jevex, now in a white tuxedo, immediately poured two large glasses of a thick, dark wine. The Duke snapped his fingers and the candles on the table lit.

"I'm glad to see we could rustle up some Devil Boy for you," the Duke said to me.

"It's finely aged, too," I said. "Real smooth."

"Only the best for my old pal."

I saw the vamp take another hit of his blood shake, and I couldn't pass up the opportunity. "So what's this I hear about an orgy?" I asked loud enough so everyone could hear.

Blood shot out of the vampire's nose like a geyser. I felt such a sense of achievement that it took a moment for me to realize that the rest of the room went silent. The creatures' eyes bore into me. They looked ready to pounce. I could swear steam was coming out of Madgogg's ears.

I looked to the Duke. He glared at me, too. Then, after a very awkward silence, he burst into laughter. Like good lackeys, the rest joined in.

"If it's sex you want, Jack, I'll introduce you to Wilma, our resident succubus."

I know a thing or two about succubi, and they're not worth the trouble. Very clingy.

"So this isn't a deviant sex club?" I said, smiling.

The Duke grinned. "We have more important things to occupy us than sex, Jack."

"Such as?"

"Such as the truth."

"Lay some truth on me, Eddie."

He stopped dead and looked at me like he wanted to rip my head off, mount it on the wall, and throw knives at it.

"I meant to say, 'Lay some truth on me, *Duke*.' "

He held his crazy eyes on me for a few more seconds. I knew to play along. I remembered that demon in the hall. He forced out a grin and said, "No harm no foul. You're just ignorant, Jack. We can't be angry at the ignorant, can we? But once you learn, then, I'm afraid, there won't be any mercy. Then you're a liability." He took a long pull of wine, and then he continued his rant. "We've all been there—stupid, uninformed, unenlightened beasts—but now we're awake, aren't we?" He raised his voice at the end of the sentence and the infernal crew jeered and shouted and agreed with their crazy lord.

He returned to normal, or the closest thing to normal he knew. "Do you know how you got here, Jack?"

"I took a boat."

He gave me a little condescending laugh. "No, I mean to Pandemonium itself."

No one really knew, but there were theories. Most of them were completely nutso. One client of mine tried to convince me we had always been here and our memories of the Other World were just illusions. I didn't subscribe to any of those theories. I said, "One day I was in the Other World and then I was here. That's the long and short of it. I stopped questioning it once I realized I wasn't going anywhere."

"Good little zombie Jack. Complacent. Obedient. Scared. Stupid."

"Maybe we're all dead and this is the afterlife."

"Is that what you believe?"

"I already died. So, wherever I go it's the afterlife." No laughs.

"I'll let you on to a little secret. It's not the afterlife. Plain and simple, Pandemonium is a prison, Jack."

"That explains the bad food." Not a chuckle. I was bombing. "So who imprisoned us? From the smirk on your face, I can tell you have an answer."

"I could never bluff this guy at poker." The Duke laughed, a bit more intensely than was comfortable, and pointed at me. "Maybe you really are a smart zombie."

"I'm not smart, just too dumb to know any better."

"You really haven't figured out who put us here and why? You fought in the war. From what I heard, you fought on both sides. Is that true, Jack?"

Now *I* was pissed. "You clearly want to make your big reveal, Duke, so let's get to it."

"Okay, Jack. It's pretty obvious. The Normals sent us here."

"The Normals? You mean people without supernatural leanings?"

"The true dead. The normal, average, unextraordinary humans

of the Other World who know only fear and hatred. The war, if you remember, was coming to a head. The Nazis were gathering supernaturals to their side, and with an army of extraordinary beings the war would be over in a flash." He snapped his fingers and the candlelight grew brighter.

I knew about the Nazis and their plans for the supernaturals all too well. I learned it firsthand in Room 731.

"But it wasn't the Nazis who sent us here," the Duke said. "It was your original side, the Allies. The scared, ignorant Americans and their lackeys."

I had never heard this. I took another hit of Devil Boy and let the formaldehyde coat my throat.

"Wasn't it your side, too?" I asked.

"I was always on *our* side." He swept out his arms to indicate all the swell folks sitting around the table. The good little toadies whooped it up and banged their fists on the table.

"Lucky us," I said.

He let that one go and continued. "The Allied Forces enlisted a group of scientists to deal with the 'supernatural problem,' as they called it. Their original plan was much worse. They wanted to commit genocide on us. Wipe us out once and for all. But we don't die so easily, do we, Jack?" I raised a glass of Devil Boy in salute. "No, they couldn't kill us, not all of us. So, they decided to banish us to another dimension, which their scientists had discovered when they were working on the atom bomb. The failed Manhattan Project. But their weak science wasn't enough to do the job. The hypocrites had to turn to a group of black magicians. They would be allowed to stay in the Other World if they could work a spell to send all the supernaturals away. It took some doing—a banishing spell like no other—but they accomplished it and—*poof!*—sent us all here to Pandemonium, an interdimensional realm that exists alongside Earth, sort of an inverted copy of the Other World." The Duke stopped, out of breath and impressed with himself. He took another long draw of wine as he waited for my next, inevitable question.

"And how do you know this, Duke?"

"That's a good question, Jack." He flashed a crazy smile. "And that reminds me of another question. Jevex, have our guests arrived?"

Something about the way he said that worried me. "You're expecting someone?" I asked.

"Three leprechauns. In fact, one is our old friend, Fine Flanagan. He's a bounty hunter now, can you believe it?"

"Sweet guy, that Flanagan." And salty, I thought as panic set in. I downed my glass and poured another. My hand trembled so badly that most of it spilled onto the table.

12

A ROOM WITHOUT A VIEW

I got lucky. The leps hadn't shown before dinner ended. Had they, what would I have done? The best I could come up with was to swear I was a different zombie. "Dead Jack who? Never heard of the brain-licker." That probably wouldn't have worked, though. I really needed to start carrying a gun.

I had tried to get the Duke to answer a few more questions, but he remained tight-lipped. He was only interested in wine and doing cheap magic tricks. At one point, he pulled a purple lizard out of my fedora. The demons ate it up. Figuratively and literally. Eventually, he excused himself from the table, saying he had more of that *business* to attend to. He offered me a room for the night and I accepted.

Jevex brought me up a marble staircase, which led to a door-lined hallway. Moonlight poked through the holes in the ceiling.

Jevex stopped at the third door on the left and opened it. He swept his clawed hand inside, indicating I should enter.

As I passed the demonic doorman, I asked, "No turndown service?" He slammed the door closed. I didn't hear a lock engage, but I also didn't hear the demon stomp away. He was no doubt guarding the door.

At least the room had an intact ceiling and solid walls. On second thought, that would make escape more difficult. The only furniture was a smashed desk and a filthy bed covered in ash and what I hoped was red wine. Dust and debris littered the floor. Flaking paint and graffiti covered the walls. In a shaky hand, someone had written "Fook Pandemonium" and "Lucifer Sucks Fairy Arse." Opposite the bed was an alcove.

When I sat on the bed, a tiny puff of ash mushroomed into the air and brimstone filled the room.

What the hell was going on here? Why was Eddie going by the Duke of Pandemonium, and why were all these demons following him like some god? When I knew him, he was a hustler and addict who couldn't hold a job. He was always trying to impress us with silly little magic tricks and his crazy ideas, but no one took him seriously. He was just another off-the-wall dust-head. Crazy Eddie had certainly moved up in the world.

I reached into my pocket before I remembered I was out of hellfire sticks. Damn! And I had forgotten to bring a bottle of Devil Boy up with me. I was pretty sure the room service in this place was for crap so I didn't try to ring up a hunchbacked bellhop.

I wasn't sure if the Duke was telling the truth about the Allies zapping us into this dimension, but I had to admit it made sense. The Nazis were definitely working with dark forces and, with their defeat seemingly imminent, they would have literally made a deal with the Devil to turn things around. Why hadn't Eddie ever mentioned this story before, though? He and I went back to the early days of Pandemonium and, at the time, he was full of wild theories. Either he had just learned of this or had kept it to himself all those years. How long was the bastard planning whatever it was he was planning?

And what did those nasty leps have to do with this? I kept thinking how every type of fairy was in that mass grave up on Corpse Hill, but not one leprechaun. Why was that? The Duke said Flanagan was in the bounty-hunting game now. That explained the overcoat and boots. But who was that winged baby that I freed in Irish Town? I had never seen anything like that little shit before. He must tie in with this. It certainly was part of the Duke's modus operandi so far: kidnapped kitties, dead fairies, a stolen Jupiter Stone.

I stood and began to pace. Where the hell could I get a pack of Lucky Dragons around here? And where the holy hell was Oswald? That little bugger better not be playing games with me. I thought for sure he'd have made an appearance by now. He was always showing up when you least expected it. How was I supposed to search the palace with Jevex tailing me? Maybe I could disguise myself and walk out backwards, making it appear that I was actually entering the room. I could throw a sheet over my head and pretend I was a ghost. I was grasping at straws.

If the leps were due at any moment, I needed to move fast.

If the bird-flipping baby had something to do with the Duke's plans, the psycho wouldn't be pleased with me freeing the tyke. The leps, on the other hand, didn't need another reason to be displeased with me. As soon as they laid eyes on me, they were going to stomp me with their little pointy shoes.

As I saw it, I didn't have many options. I either had to slip past Jevex or fight him to the death.

Bzzt-bzzt. Bzzt-bzzt. Bzzt-bzzt.

A demonic fly zipped across my nose.

"Hey, arsehole!" it said.

A second infernal insect buzzed in my ear.

"Think we forgot about you, corpse?"

A third black bugger bit me on the neck.

I swatted at them and they dispersed. They regrouped and hovered in V-formation just out of reach.

"That was an ugly thing you did to Carl," one of them said. I think it was the middle one. His bony horns pointed at my face. "Swatting him like a common housefly."

"The indignity!"

"The injustice!"

"The iniquity!"

"He had it coming," I said. "Just like the rest of you."

I pulled out my lighter, flicked it on, and jabbed it at them. The infernal insects flew off.

"He's a madman!" one of them shouted.

"Murderer!" another yelled.

"He'll burn the lot of us, the sicko!"

"Bite his eyes!"

"Blind the fooker!"

The demonic flies came at me from all directions. *Bzzt-bzzt. Bzzt-bzzt. Bzzt-bzzt.* I had a surprise for them. I pulled off my hat and swiped it at the three buggers. The blast of air sent them into the alcove. I ran after them with my lighter blazing.

"I'm going to roast you!" I shouted. "Slowly!"

"You heard that, Jasper?"

"He's a sadist, he is!"

"How isn't this guy locked up on Purgatory Island?"

The dumb demons were trapped. I stood in the entry to the alcove. The three flies sat on the far wall.

I turned up the flame.

"He's serious," a fly piped.

"Be brave, lads. He ain't got us yet."

"First I'm going to cook you," I said, "and then I'm going to eat you."

"A damn ghoul!"

"Sweet Lucifer, why did we mess with this monster?"

"We're coming to meet you, Carl. Keep a seat warm for us in Hell."

I leapt at the demonic flies, my lighter leading the charge. I don't know if I killed any of them, but I absolutely murdered the wall. My hand went right through it, the stone crumbling like it was made of dust and spit. With nothing to brace myself, my head collided with the wall. That's all it needed to fall apart. The wall crumbled—and I kept going. I was hoping I had uncovered a hidden passageway, but all I found was a shaft that led straight down.

The *Broken* Palace? The dump was falling apart.

I must have dropped a hundred feet. My head thought it was a pinball banging off the bumpers, except here the bumpers were stone walls.

I dropped into a space narrower than a preacher's mind.

Claustrophobia isn't a problem for the undead. In fact, the tighter the space the more at home I feel. And the dark? Well, I was always more comfortable in the dark than the light. Probably that had to do with my handsome face. So, I wasn't panicking. Yet.

My feet weren't touching the ground. I tried to shimmy, but I only managed a slight wiggle. I was wedged in pretty good. I tried sucking in my gut, but that didn't help. The only thing I could move was my head, but only about an inch or two back and forth.

Cold and damp wrapped around my bones. I was pretty sure I was underneath the palace. I sure dropped far enough.

I couldn't see anything. My lighter must have flown out of my hand when I took that tumble through the wall.

If my head was hard enough to bash through the alcove, maybe I could do the same here.

I head-butted the wall. Unfortunately, the stone below the palace was in much better shape. I did manage to blow the dust off the wall and into my eyes. I was going to have the headache to end all headaches, but I wasn't too keen on waiting a few hundred years for the palace to fall down around me on its own.

I pulled back my head until it touched the back wall and let it rip. The first few strikes did nothing, but the other three dozen or so did the trick. Dust and mortar filled the air and slowly the stone bricks moved. When I saw a fraction of light seep through, I re-doubled my efforts. I chipped a tooth.

Once one brick fell, the others were no trouble. I demolished the wall and, with the grace of an ice-skating ogre, I slipped through it.

13

BENEATH THE PALACE
OF THE ARSEHOLES

I stood in a cramped storage room. Wooden barrels lined the right wall. Most had been smashed open and emptied. Bare shelves hung to my left.

I shivered in the underground cold.

I found the door, which opened onto a hallway dimly lit by torches in niches. My footsteps echoed against the stone floor. The hall led to other halls and passageways of rough stone walls and low-arched ceilings. Soon I was lost.

I searched for one of those maps that say "You Are Here!" I had no such luck. But then I came upon a steel door that seemed particularly important, mostly because there was a sign on it that read: STAY OUT!

It was locked, as you would expect for a door with a STAY

OUT sign, but there wasn't a lock in Pandemonium I couldn't pick.

I went to remove my lock-picking tools from my breast pocket—actually, it's a paper clip. Or I would have, if it was still there. Most likely my trusty paper clip now resided at the bottom of the Broken Sea.

I kicked the door. It didn't open.

I tried the door handle again. No, it was definitely locked.

An overturned tin pail sat in a corner. In my frustration, I kicked the stupid bucket, mostly for the joke of it. My foot got stuck in the wire handle and I fell. So much for jokes. As I bemoaned my fate, I had a brilliant idea. I grabbed the bucket and pulled off the handle. The wire was—I hoped—thin enough to fit inside the lock.

I straightened the handle as best I could and jammed it inside the lock. Delicately, I worked it inside the mechanism until I heard that satisfying *click*.

The door opened.

Unlike the rest of the underground level, here the ceiling was high and the room as wide as a ShadowShade block. Maybe the place had once been a dungeon—shackles were bolted into the walls—but now it looked like a madman's laboratory. Electronics and wires covered benches. Machines big and small were scattered around the room. Some even had blinking lights, so I knew they were high-tech. But the most interesting features were in the center, where four large glass containers stood in a semi-circle. As I got closer, I could see that each held something or someone.

Immediately I was reminded of the glass jar that held Flanagan's insolent baby. But these were much bigger, at least ten feet high.

I crouched in the shadows.

The vessels held human-looking creatures—human except for the folded-up wings at their backs. They were naked and tall and ill-looking. Sickly black and red spots covered their dull, gray skin. Their heads sat heavy on their shoulders. They seemed to be sleeping on their feet. I also noticed that there was nothing where their genitals should have been, just a smooth piece of skin.

Seeing these poor creatures filled me with an incredible sense of sadness. I was overcome by emotion and—this is hard to admit—I was on the verge of tears. I was pretty sure my tear ducts wouldn't produce any tears, but my body wanted them to erupt.

Sticking to the shadows, I crept up to the closest vessel. I gently tapped on the glass, like an obnoxious tourist at an aquarium.

"I wouldn't do that if I were you."

I jumped, but tried to look suave as I turned. I think I pulled it off.

The Duke emerged from the opposite side of the room.

"Jack, I should have warned you not to wander around the palace. There are things here you won't understand."

"You got me there. This place is a real head-scratcher."

One of the creatures lifted its head and looked in my direction. His—her?—silver eyes seemed to be pleading with me. A lump formed in my throat. I had to turn away.

"It's a long story, my friend. Come with me and I'll tell you all about it."

I looked back at the creature, but its head was slumped like the others.

The Duke led me into a small side room, which resembled a typical ShadowShade office with a desk and chairs and bookcases. The books, however, weren't typical. Enochian script covered most of the spines. The Duke opened a desk drawer and pulled out a bottle of Devil Boy, a bottle of whiskey, and two glasses. He poured me a glass of Devil Boy and the whiskey for himself. He sat. I didn't.

"Are they that *business* you needed to attend to?" I asked.

"In a manner of speaking."

"What are they?"

"Our ticket out of Pandemonium."

"That's your plan? To escape and return to the Other World?"

"What other plan is there? Pandemonium is a prison."

"You said that before."

"You believe it, don't you?"

"I don't care."

"You're a fool, Jack."

"Then enlighten me. How are those poor bastards going to get you out of Pandemonium? Fly you out of here?" He took a hit of whiskey and I did the same with the Devil Boy. It wasn't as good as the stuff I had at dinner, but it wasn't bad.

"I wish it were that easy. You see, I've been looking for a way out of this hell the second I landed here. You asked me how I knew about the Pandemonium Project."

"Did you use a scryer? You know they're all a scam, right?"

"I know because I was part of Project Pandemonium. I was one of the dark magicians who cast the banishment spell."

That answered that. I poured myself another Devil Boy, drank it down in one gulp. "And you messed it up and got yourself sent here?"

"No. I was double-crossed."

"I guess you can't trust dark magicians, can you?"

"No. You cannot. And me most of all. You see, I had planned to double-cross *them*." The Duke laughed and flashed his crazy eyes. "Don't you get it, Jack? Those magicians would be the *only* supernaturals left in the Other World after the banishment. The government would have to keep them happy, too, because they'd need them to get rid of any *new* supernaturals. They would be set up for *life*. *Gods* among *men*. But if there were *any* supernaturals in the Other World, there was always the chance of someone honing in on your action, right? So, I figured I'd banish the other two and rule the world myself. It would have been fookin sweet."

"But they figured it out because you're you, and they voilà'd your arse here, too?"

"The best laid plans..."

"So why don't you just cast a spell to get yourself out of here?"

The Duke lowered his head. For the first time ever, he seemed reticent. He stroked his whiskey glass. "Jack, this can't get out. To anyone. You understand?"

"You can trust me, Eddie—I mean the Duke."

"No. It's all right, Jack. We're old friends. That Duke business is for the crowd upstairs. Down here I'm just plain ol' Eddie McCrawley, ShadowShade hustler. Remember that time we got arrested for stealing Lucifer's goats?" I did. I spent two nights on Purgatory Island before I could make bail. Eddie never set foot on the prison island. I never knew what he did to pull that off.

He seemed to be lost in thought. "What was it you were going to tell me?" I asked.

Without looking at me, he said, "I don't have any powers in Pandemonium. Never have. Those two bastards bound my abilities. It wasn't enough that they sent me to another dimension." The Duke threw his glass of whiskey across the room. It shattered against the wall.

I ignored the outburst. "But I've seen you do magic."

"Illusions. Parlor tricks. It's all bullshit to keep up appearances. I'm probably the weakest person in Pandemonium. The most ordinary person here."

"You've done quite well for yourself considering."

He smiled wickedly. Like a vampire who's just cornered a red-blooded virgin. "I have a knowledge advantage. I knew a little about this dimension before I got here. I began searching for answers, learning, and finally I discovered their existence." He pointed at the open door.

"Those things in the glass tubes?"

"The interdimensional beings."

"IDBs." Something clicked in my rotten head. The leps were looking for an IDB back in Irish Town.

"They are the original inhabitants of Pandemonium. Beings

that can travel as easily between dimensions as you and I travel from one room to another. Once I learned of their existence, I set out to contact them. I figured they could transport me back to the Other World, but the beings aren't concerned with humans or much else. They ignored me. Never acknowledged my existence. Even after I captured them. I've had some of them for decades and not a peep. I begged and bribed the bastards, but they wouldn't help me. Nothing worked. Not until I *tortured* them."

The way the word *tortured* rolled off his tongue gave me a chill. I remembered the dead kobold's words. "The interdimensional ones hurt." He was sure right about that.

"They still didn't talk," the Duke said, "but I got the answer I needed anyway. Hurting them hurts Pandemonium. They are *connected* to this place. Perhaps they even *are* it. I'm not sure, and it doesn't matter."

"I still don't see how you'll get out of Pandemonium."

"It's quite simple. I destroy all the interdimensional beings, I destroy Pandemonium. I have a device." His eyes grew wild. The Duke really had lost his mind.

I still wasn't getting it. "Wouldn't that destroy you and the rest of us, too?"

"Yes." He smirked. One hundred percent bonkers.

"That's how you get out of Pandemonium? Kill yourself?"

"I'll be protected."

That's when it hit me. "The cats!"

"That's why you're here, isn't it? I smelled the goblin on you immediately. Cats are natural interdimensional beings. But they're too uncaring to help anyone but themselves. That must be a thing with IDBs. Believe me, I've tried. It doesn't matter. Their blood will work fine. Once we destroy Pandemonium, we need only to drink the cat's fresh blood and we'll be safe."

"Sounds like a hell of a plan." I didn't know what part of it sounded crazier. I kept the knowledge of the Jupiter Stone to myself, but I was pretty sure what he needed it for.

"There's one more piece," the Duke said. This kept getting better. I figured I'd just play along and hopefully find Oswald, rescue the cats, and hightail it out of the psych ward before he caught on. "The fifth and last interdimensional being will be delivered to me tonight. Then it's bye-bye, Pandemonium."

Someone was going to be very disappointed. That bird-flipping interdimensional baby was long gone. What a genius move on my part, setting him free. I reminded myself to rub it in Oswald's face.

"You can come with us, Jack. We're not just going back to the Old World. We're going to conquer it."

"I'm not much of the conquering type. Pandemonium may be a prison, but it's home to me. Hell sweet hell."

"I knew you'd say that, Jack. You never had many aspirations or any imagination. Kind of a low-hanging-fruit guy. But what should I expect from a soulless zombie?"

I rolled my eyes. I'd heard that approximately a billion times in my life. "Then why would you tell a loser like me your nefarious plans? Seems a bit unwise."

"Because, Jack, you are about to forget everything I told you." He held up the bottle of Devil Boy and winked.

"Fook."

"Yeah, and it gets better."

The Duke's gaze rose over my head to about the height of an orc hitman. An orc I had no doubt was behind me and about to land a very meaty orc fist onto my skull.

Then things got the opposite of better.

14

A ZOMBIE
BY ANY OTHER NAME

My head felt like a balloon filled with two tons of lead. I was sure it was going to rip off my shoulders. Actually, I prayed it would.

The world blurred and spun like a mad merry-go-round. I shut my eyes, but the spinning continued. I think I puked.

Gradually, my vision cleared and the world slowed. But my troubles were only beginning. I had no idea where I was. That was par for the course because I had no idea *who* I was either.

I was in a strange room. (Naturally.) But other than the fact that I had never seen it before, it was strange because the torches on the wall pointed down. That couldn't be right. I looked around as best I could with my lead-filled head. To my left was a wall of bars. I was in a *prison*? I didn't remember committing a crime, but then again I didn't remember *not* committing a crime.

I noticed something else inside the small cell. A woman. She stood on the ceiling and hung straight down like a bat.

"How are you doing that?" I asked, and was startled by the sound of my voice, which seemed to croak like, well, something that croaked. My ability to form similes seemed compromised by my lack of knowing...stuff.

"Doing what?" the woman responded. She wore her black hair in pigtails, but somehow they didn't hang down as you would expect for an upside-down person. They pointed up toward the ceiling. She also wore a straitjacket.

"How are you standing like that on the ceiling? Are you a witch?"

She looked at me like I was speaking gibberish.

"I *am* a witch actually," she said, "but I'm standing perfectly normally."

I must have fallen asleep and woken up in some upside-down world. I didn't know if that type of thing happened, but again I was short on knowledge.

"What is the name of this world?" I asked. It was probably something like Topsy-Turvy or Up Is Down or Down Is Up.

"Pandemonium."

"Never heard of it. Does Pandemonium mean something like Upside-Down World?"

She smiled, though it actually looked like a grin. "I think I see your dilemma. You're the one upside down."

She was right. I finally looked at my feet. They were strapped to the wall, as were my hands and chest.

"Do you know how I got here?" I asked.

"I assume you pissed off the Duke. The dirty, rotten, lying, piece of scum that he is."

"I wonder what I did to piss him off."

"Oh, it doesn't take much. Believe me. I'm surprised he didn't kill you."

"Why did he put you in that straitjacket?"

"So I can't do any magic. I need to use my hands and I usually need blood."

"No, I meant why are you in here? How did you piss off the Duke?"

"I could tell you, but what the fook difference would it make? You don't know anything. I'd probably have to explain a bunch of basic stuff, like what a man is and what a piece of scum is and how a man can lie to your face for years and we'd be here all day."

"Aren't we going to be here all day regardless?"

"I'd still rather not."

"Could you at least tell me why I don't know anything?"

"You probably didn't know much to begin with since you're a zombie."

I screamed. Then I went silent. I tried to listen for a heartbeat. There wasn't one. I looked closer at my hands. The left one looked terrible. It was nearly all bone like a skeleton hand. The right hand didn't look much better.

"Sorry to break it to you," the witch said. "But for what it's worth, you seem like a top-notch zombie. I mean, I've never met one who didn't just moan and try to eat flesh, and I used to spend a lot of time on the Zombie Islands as a kid."

I did feel a stirring in my guts and a craving for the witch's flesh, but I kept that to myself.

"Even if I am a zombie, I feel like I should know how I got here or what I did yesterday."

"From the looks of it, and the smell of you, I'd say you were bathing in fish guts yesterday. But you don't remember most likely because the Duke slipped you water from the River Lethe. It wipes your memory. He loves using the stuff."

"How do you know the Duke?"

"I was kind of his girlfriend. So stupid. I should have listened to my father, but the Duke comes off as a pretty cool dude, and he looks damn good in that tunic."

"Any chance of you two getting back together?"

"You know, when you wind up in a straitjacket in a jail cell in your ex-boyfriend's dungeon, any chance of reconciliation is probably off the table. Unless he brings me flowers, then I'd totally be his again."

"Really?"

"No, you idiot. I hate flowers."

"I don't know how I feel about flowers."

"I don't mean to be rude, but I'm not used to having a cellmate and I kind of enjoy my solitude. Besides, I think I'm close to dislocating my shoulder, so I can finally get out of this strait-jacket. If you don't mind, please shut the fook up." She sat on the ground and began to rock back and forth as she wiggled her shoulders.

She seemed to mean it, so I shut up. I used the quiet time to try remembering basic things about myself. Like my name.

Zilch. Where I was from. Nada. How I got there. Uh-uh. Where here was. No dice. Why I was so hungry. How I became a zombie. Why I smelled like seawater and dead fish. My mind was a blank. I had a strong feeling my head was literally empty. That didn't give me much confidence in my situation. When the white blob slithered under the prison bars, my confidence sunk even lower. If things like that existed in this world, I was happy I didn't remember.

15

RETURN OF THE
WHITE BLOB

The white blob flowed toward me like a puddle of spilled milk on a mission. I screamed. The witch stopped trying to dislocate her shoulder, jumped up, and backed away from the ooze.

What the hell is that?" she said.

The living puddle came to rest underneath my head. I tried to pull away, but there wasn't much give in my restraints. I watched as the puddle coalesced and rose into a cone. A tiny head popped into existence, then two legs and two arms. Finally, two X's appeared on his head and a slit formed for a mouth. The thing wore an expression on its newly constructed face. It was an unpleasant expression.

"Well, well, well," the little creature said in an irritating little voice. "Look at you. I should leave you here. It would serve you right after what you pulled. 'I bet you can't turn yourself into a cat, Oswald.' 'Go farther out.' 'Frolic, Oswald!' Ha, ha, ha. Was that your brilliant plan? What was supposed to happen after the demon caught me, huh? You really are an idiot, you know that?" The former puddle of milk put his little hands on his little hips. After a moment, it said, "Not going to say anything?"

"You talking to me, little guy?" I asked.

The creature's X-shaped eyes turned into O's almost the size of its head.

"I'm talking to the only idiot in this room."

"What are you, if I may ask?"

"What am I? I'm the partner of a self-centered idiot. I guess that makes me an idiot, too, but you know what? I'm free and you're chained to a wall, upside down. Too bad you don't have any blood to rush to your head."

"You know me? How do you know me?"

"Ha, ha. Has the dust finally rotted what's left of your brain? Well, if you're going to play it like that, I *will* leave you here. Teach you a lesson. I know where the cats are, by the way. I'm sure I can rescue them myself, and then I'll get the reward from the goblins and be the hero for once."

"Buddy, his memory has been compromised," the witch said. "The Duke gave him the water of forgetfulness."

The blob turned toward the witch. "Isn't that convenient? He throws me to the demons and now I can't even nag him about it."

"Look, you can do whatever you want with your friend, but I'd appreciate it if you got me out of here first."

"This guy doesn't appreciate anything I do, and if he'd just listen to me we'd both be better off. His idea of a plan—"

"Listen, I don't care about your dysfunctional relationship. We shouldn't be wasting any time. Get me out of here and I can help you get your friend's memory back."

"I don't know if I want that. He might be better off like this."

I didn't like this sassy pipsqueak, but he might be the only thing that had any idea who I was. "Little blob," I said, "I don't remember anything about you, but I will remember this."

The creature turned its head and seemed to be in thought. Its X eyes blinked twice. "All right, all right," he said finally. "I was going to free you. I just wanted to make you suffer a bit."

The little man extended his right hand, which then formed into a pick. He inserted it into the lock holding my head to the wall. After a few seconds, I heard a *click* and the lock opened. My head was free! I tried moving it, but it was damn sore. The bones in my neck popped like popcorn on a hot stove. The little guy went to work on the other locks and soon I came crashing to the ground. My head cushioned the fall.

I stood and it took a few seconds to adjust to the room being right side up. I needed to steady myself against the wall. As I tried to get the room to stop spinning, the blob freed the witch.

She seemed much taller now that we were both right side up. In fact, she was at least a few inches taller than me. She was broad-shouldered and had thick muscular legs. She obviously did calisthenics. With the jacket off, I could now see that tattoos—intricate sigils and random objects—covered her arms. A large sledgehammer took up most of her right arm. She wore a black sleeveless shirt with the words "Fook Off" written across her chest. I didn't know if freeing her was a good idea.

"The water of memory is on the other side of the palace," the witch said to me. "I hope you didn't forget how to fight."

"Trust me, he never knew how," the blob said and laughed. It sounded like an idiot bird chirping.

"I'll only go," I said, "if you make sure I never remember this tiny creature." The blob dropped its shoulders and hung his head. I think I hurt the little guy's feelings.

16

A STROLL DOWN MNEMOSYNE LANE

As we approached the cell door, demonic snoring stopped us in our tracks. We froze like ghouls caught eating their best friend's corpse.

"Sorry. I forgot the guard," the blob said. "I had no problem slipping past him on account of him sleeping, but I don't think the three of us can just saunter by."

"I got this," the witch said and then sliced her palm with a fingernail, drawing blood. "You," she said to the blob, "come here!"

"My name is Oswald."

"Okay, Oswald, I'm Zara Moonbeam. Now that we're all friends—"

"That sounds like a pixie name."

"I'm half-pixie."

"Which half?" I asked.

"I'm kind of sensitive about my size," Zara Moonbeam said. "And when I get sensitive, people usually get hurt."

She looked at me with psycho eyes, wide and focused. Her tattoos seemed to ripple. This woman meant business.

"I must have forgotten my manners, too," I said and took a step back.

"You never had any," Oswald said.

I shot the blob a dirty look. "Hey, since we're on the topic of names, what's mine?"

"Jack," Oswald said.

"I like that. I knew I had a strong masculine name. Not like Oswald."

"He loses his memory," Oswald said, "but he's exactly the same."

"Will you two cut it out?" Zara said. "Oz, I need you to slip back out there and not have the demon notice you. Can you do that?"

"Not being noticed is what I do best."

"First, I need you to form one of your hands into a stylus or something to write with."

"Like this?" The blob held up its right arm, which was now as thin as a pencil and sharp at the end.

"Perfect. Now dab the tip in my blood. Get it good and bloody. Then slip out there and draw a circle around that demon. It'll trap him. We'll be able to walk right by him."

Oswald dipped his pencil hand in the blood, walked to the bars, flattened himself like a pancake, and slid out of the cell.

"You sure this will work?" I asked.

"I've done this many times before. I know my way around demons."

I believed her. She seemed like she could handle herself against anything, but I had my doubts about the blob. I couldn't imagine why I would know such a weird and disrespectful creature. He certainly didn't seem like anyone I'd want to befriend. I must be a desperate zombie with pals like that.

The demon had apparently woken up or was having the mother of all nightmares, because he was yelling bloody murder. Then he began stomping. The cell bars rattled.

The door swung open and there was Oswald, smirking. "It worked! Come on!"

I looked at Zara. She shrugged.

Outside the cell, we were met by a very irate demon. Smoke puffed out of his flared nostrils and ears. His eyes burned red.

"I will make you pay dearly for this," the demon said and slammed his clawed feet into the floor.

The blob did a pretty poor job of drawing that magic circle, if you ask me. It was barely a circle, more like a demented hexagon. The demon lunged at us, but bounced back when he hit the edge of the blood line.

"This way," Zara said and led us down the hall. We turned left, and then right, and went through a door, which opened onto a winding stone staircase.

We made it about three steps when we heard the distinct snap of demon wings.

"The circle must have had a gap!" Zara said.

I glared at Oswald.

"What?!" he said.

Hot air rushed toward us.

"Go!" Zara yelled, and we ran up the staircase.

The demon was on the stairs in no time. We slipped around the first bend. The creature tried to navigate the narrow opening, but crashed into the wall and went tumbling down the stairs.

"I am going to eat your souls," the demon barked when he regained his footing.

"The joke is on you!" Oswald shouted back. "We don't have souls!"

"Speak for yourselves," Zara said.

This seemed to anger the demon. He howled, and the stink of his hot breath made us gag. The beast's bony feet slapped against the stone as he climbed the stairs in giant leaps.

"My memory isn't great," I said, "but I'm sure zombies aren't great runners. Sooner or later, he's going to catch me."

"Let me handle this," Oswald said, and the little blob melted into a puddle. I hopped over him.

Zara had stopped running and was waiting several steps above me.

"Keep going," I said. "The demon isn't far behind."

She ran her fingertips over her right arm and mumbled something in a strange, lilting language. I couldn't believe what I was seeing. She lifted the sledgehammer tattoo off her arm and a real sledgehammer appeared in her hand. Except this one was half the size of Zara herself.

The demon bellowed as he crashed onto the steps, most likely after slipping on Oswald. The sound of claws scraping against the stone walls made me cringe.

"Get behind me," Zara said, and I did.

She held up the sledgehammer. The demon came stomping up the staircase, smoke spewing out of his mouth and nostrils. When he saw Zara, his expression went from furious to "oh fook."

It was the last expression he'd ever make. The witch/pixie swung for the fences, connecting the head of the sledgehammer with the head of the demon, which smashed against the wall. Bits of demon skull and stone pelted us.

Zara slid the sledgehammer back toward her arm and it was a tattoo again.

"You'll have to give me the name of your tattoo artist," I said.

"I did it myself actually," she said.

Oswald had re-formed into a cocky little man and joined us. Maybe the little blob wasn't so bad after all.

"Let's get going," Zara said. "The other demons will have heard that and will be on us soon enough."

As we hustled up the stairs, Zara told us that the two rivers the Duke discovered on Monster Island were called Lethe and Mnemosyne, or the rivers of forgetfulness and memory. He kept bottles of the waters in a special storeroom.

"But won't that be heavily guarded?" I asked.

"Of course," Zara said.

"And you think we can take on an army of demons?"

"Who? A dead guy and a shape-shifting marshmallow?"

"We did all right just now."

"We? Don't worry about an army of demons. I'm taking you to my quarters. I stole a few vials of the waters."

At the top of the stairs was a landing with several doors. Zara opened the third one and we entered a long, narrow hallway. We followed Zara through several other hallways until we reached a gold door. There was no handle or doorknob on it.

"How do you get inside?" I asked.

"Magic, of course," she said. "That's how I know the room is as I kept it. No one but me can get in."

Zara mumbled something in that weird language, and then traced a tattoo of a gold key on her left arm. She mumbled more cryptic words and the key appeared in her hand. The tattoo was gone, her brown skin now in its place.

When Zara placed the key near the door, a keyhole appeared. She put the key in the lock and opened the door.

Everything inside was black. The walls, the ceiling, the floor, the rugs, the furniture—everything beside the posters and pictures of something called Kill Unicorn Kill. They looked like a swing band full of psychos.

"You really like black," I said.

"It likes me," Zara said and put the key back on her arm. I had no idea what that meant. "I'll be right back," she said and went through a door on her right.

I was alone with the little creature.

He glared at me.

"What's this about cats?" I asked.

"That's why we're here. To rescue the cats and bring them back to the goblins."

"Why would I do that?"

"Mainly for fairy dust. You're a detective, Jack."

"A zombie detective? Sounds like a stupid idea."

"It pays the bills."

"Am I any good at it?"

"Well...let's say things usually work out in the end."

"And how do we know each other?"

"I used to live inside your skull. Now I'm your partner. Your *equal* partner."

"You're a strange one, Oswald."

"Wait till you remember."

I didn't like the way he said that. I wasn't sure getting my memory back was a good thing. I figured if you were a zombie, you must have messed up big time in your past.

Zara returned with a large box. Naturally, it was black.

She placed it on a table beside us and opened the lid. Inside were two glass jars. One was filled with a milky white liquid and the other with a dark, cloudy liquid. Zara removed the jar with white liquid and popped it open.

"Is that okay to drink?" I asked.

"I think this is what made the Duke insane or, I should say, more insane," she said. "He was always a bit off. Long after he found the rivers, he continued to drink water from Mnemosyne. Eventually, he remembered everything in his life all the way back to the womb, everything anyone had ever said to him, anything he had overheard or read. I think it broke his mind."

Zara dipped her finger inside the container and held it up to me. "Okay, drink this."

"You were never a salesman, were you?" I asked.

"It's fine. I've taken it before. The Duke tricked me into drinking from the water of forgetfulness after our fallout, but I was ready for him." She held up the back of her right hand, where she had tattooed the word "DRINK" and an image of a shot glass. "I just needed to lift out the glass and drink."

"Clever," I said.

"I'll give you only a drop at a time, until we get your memory back to where it was."

"Are you sure you want to do it that way?" Oswald asked. "He is a zombie after all."

"If he so much as takes a peck, I think he knows what I'll do. Right, Jack?"

I looked at the sledgehammer tattoo that almost ran the length of her right arm. "I have some ideas," I said and delicately licked the water off Zara's fingertip. Immediately, something in my head popped, like a flash grenade going off in my skull.

"What is your oldest memory?" Zara asked.

I searched my brain. "Meeting the goblin queen."

Oswald grinned.

Zara gave me another drop of memory juice. "What do you remember now?"

I hesitated and rubbed my hands on my thighs. I thought about lying, but I was afraid Oswald would call me out. "Eating a leprechaun," I mumbled.

"What was that?" Zara asked.

"Eating a leprechaun," I said more clearly.

"You ate a leprechaun? A little, defenseless leprechaun?"

"They aren't so defenseless, you know!"

Zara grimaced and dabbed her finger again. We kept at it for maybe another two dozen times. I remembered Oswald oozing out of my skull all those years ago; my arrival in Pandemonium; having my soul stolen from me; Room 731; Ratzinger; fighting in the war; and my pre-zombie life, which had been mostly a blur before the Duke slipped me the water of forgetfulness. But now long-lost memories flooded back and I wanted nothing more than to stuff them back in the darkness. When visions of a blonde woman with green eyes appeared in my mind, I stopped Zara. "No more," I said. "I remember enough. We're good. Put the water away."

She closed the jar and returned it to the box.

"How does it feel to have your memory back?" Oswald asked.

"It's not going to feel good for you. I remember how you never filed a report for the Purloined Unicorn case eight years ago."

"Crap. I had forgotten about that."

"We'll deal with that later. Where are the cats?"

"The cats are gone."

"Gone? Why didn't you say something sooner?"

"What was the point? You didn't have any memory."

"Do you know where they are, dunzy?"

"The Duke took off with them."

"Great! The Duke is gone, too."

"I have more bad news."

"You're on a roll."

"I saw the two leprechauns from Irish Town here. The Duke was really pissed with them. Then they took off for Monster Island with most of the other lackeys from the palace. They were carrying a bunch of equipment. Looks like they were preparing for something big. Why are the leps here, Jack?"

"To make my life miserable. I'll explain everything on the way to Monster Island."

17

A GOD REBORN

Oswald was right. (There's a first time for everything.) Most of the palace had been evacuated. On our way out, we slipped past a few demons and vampires. They were too busy getting drunk and horsing around to notice us. The Duke apparently left behind the losers. Maybe to mop up and meet the Duke on Monster Island, or maybe he abandoned them to their fate like us.

I figured the only reason he left me and Ms. Moonbeam in the cell instead of killing us was because we'd die soon enough once he destroyed the IDBs. Why waste time trying to kill a member of the undead and a witch who'd put up a hell of a fight?

I didn't check, but I was sure the interdimensional beings were gone, too. The Duke must have been heading to Monster Island to catch the last IDB and kill them all right there. He wasn't going to leave anything to chance now.

We made our way out of the palace through an underground tunnel that Zara knew about. Or we almost made it out. Just feet from the exit, we ran into that ancient vampire I met at dinner.

"The smart zombie," he said. "So, you're not dead. I mean truly dead. Because you've always been kinda dead, right?" He slurred his words and wobbled. He was clearly drunk.

"What was your name again?" I asked.

"Count Ardlin, at your service." He tried to bow but stumbled instead.

"Why didn't you go with the Duke to Monster Island?"

"I guess I wasn't invited." He hiccupped and a trickle of blood dripped out of his nose. "Or maybe I had been partying too hard to notice he had gone. That succubus Wilma is a real doll. Maybe I'll catch a water taxi. Hey, aren't you the Duke's bitch?" He looked at Zara.

She wasted no time. She spoke the strange words and grabbed her sledgehammer tattoo. The vampire didn't even have time to blink. Zara took three quick giant steps, and then lowered the boom onto his head, which burst like a watermelon filled with firecrackers. I got a bit more blood on me and a vampire fang lodged in my neck. I had a tough time pulling it out.

"I think we can go now," I said. "Unless Zara wants to bash in a few more heads."

She seemed to think about it, and then said, "I'm good."

We exited the palace and I had never been so happy to see the red skies of Pandemonium. I could have kissed it. We weren't far from the shore so we decided to head there. We had no idea how we'd get to Monster Island, but I was damn sure a ghost ship wouldn't be involved.

On the way, we pieced together the Duke's plan.

I told Zara about the winged baby we encountered in Irish Town. "That insolent brat is all the Duke needs to destroy Pandemonium and everyone in it," I said. "The leps must have been on their way to deliver it to the Duke when I messed up their plan."

"Why would the leps be involved?" Oswald asked. "Why wouldn't the Duke capture the baby himself?"

"Probably because the Duke doesn't have any powers. His magic was bound when the other black magicians sent him to Pandemonium." Zara looked at me in disbelief. "You didn't know?"

"That piece of filth," she said. "I should have known, but he's a damn good liar. He needed the water of memory to compensate for his lack of magical powers. That's how he come up with the plans for the device."

"What device?" Oswald asked.

"He calls it the Pandemonium Device. It's equipped with a Jupiter Stone. It's the only way he can kill the IDBs."

I had figured as much.

"But how do they know the baby is on Monster Island?" Oswald asked. "Why wouldn't he be able to move between dimensions?"

"Simple," Zara said. "The leps must have put binding and tracking spells on him. They're crafty, which is why the Duke used them. Leps know a thing or two about moving between dimensions themselves."

"That leaves the cats," Oswald said. "Why did the Duke take them?"

I fielded that one. "The Duke believes their blood will protect them when Pandemonium is destroyed. So how are we getting to Monster Island? Zara, is your witchcraft capable of transporting us there?"

"If I had my broom, I could have flown us. But I must have misplaced it."

"You should keep a backup."

"Never had a broom. That's a myth. I was joking."

"This isn't the time for jokes."

A warm blast of air hit us and I nearly fell over. Heavy wings whooshed overhead.

"Find cover!" I shouted. "The demons are attacking!"

The three of us ran toward a grouping of stones and ducked behind them.

Laughter filled the air. Demonic laughter. Like something you'd hear in the deepest pits of Hell as you're being worked over by Lucifer.

Zara grabbed her sledgehammer, Oswald got into a fighting stance, and I adjusted my hat. The demon buzzed us again, shooting past us just overhead. I caught a glimpse of the creature's wings as he flew away from us. They must have been twenty feet wide.

When the demon circled back, I got a better look at him. I instantly noticed the distinct burn marks on the creature's body. That was no demon. It was Camazotz.

"Hey, Camazotz! Camazotz!" I shouted.

"Pipe down, you idiot," Zara said. "He'll hear you."

"I know him. He saved my life before." I stood and waved my arms. Zara grabbed me and pulled me down to the ground.

"Are you crazy? That's the guy who stole the Jupiter Stone."

The bat god swooped low, angling toward us. He was coming in fast. For a moment, I had forgotten that he ditched me on Corpse Hill and stole my dust. Crap, the dust! He must be high as a kite. He probably doesn't even remember me.

"Maybe I miscalculated," I said. Then I remembered something else. Camazotz didn't have wings.

The giant bat flew right into me, knocking me down. Zara lifted her sledgehammer. I jumped up. "Camazotz?" I asked. "Is that you?" He did say he was one of a kind.

The giant bat perched himself on top of a large stone, his wings fully spread out. There was something strange about them.

"Jack!" he shouted. "Just the dead man I wanted to see."

"You really do know this guy?" Zara asked, but she didn't lower her sledgehammer.

"I think so," I said. "Camazotz, buddy, what's going on? Your wings grew back?"

He was beaming. At first I thought it was because of the dust I had given him, but he didn't have that glazed look in his eyes.

"No," he said. "I bought them."

"I thought you had nothing to your name."

"I didn't. Not before you gave me that dust. Do you know how valuable that stuff is?"

I was thinking maybe I overpaid for his help.

"I gave Gandall the Tinkerer the dust, and he fixed me up with these canvas wings."

"Are they as good as the real things?"

Camazotz laughed and flapped his wings, sending a blast of air in our direction almost as powerful as Zara's sledgehammer.

"Okay, okay," I said. "We get the point."

"I am reborn," Camazotz said, standing straighter than an arrow. "Camazotz the Thief is back!"

"Listen, Zotzy," I said. "How would you like more dust?"

18

FLYING THE
FIENDISH SKIES

The bat god had no problem carrying the three of us. He was so jacked up on good vibes, I think he could have circumnavigated Pandemonium with three pregnant krakens on his back.

We worked out the matter of the stolen Jupiter Stone before we boarded Air Camazotz. He swore he knew nothing about the dead fairies before he took the job to steal the stone. When he did find out, he tried to return the stone. But the Duke caught him and, as punishment, used the stone to burn his wings and other parts of his body. Zara corroborated the story.

Oswald the diva, on the other hand, had big problems. I keep the obnoxious homunculus around because he occasionally comes in handy, and this time he came in extremely handy.

I had Oswald stretch himself into a hammock, which we tied

to Camazotz's tail on one end and around his neck on the other. Zara and I got in the hammock, and we all flew toward Monster Island. It was quite comfortable, I have to admit. Bat god first class.

There was a lovely view, which I might have enjoyed if Oswald had stopped complaining.

"A ghost ship would have been better than this," he chirped. "You two are much heavier than I thought. I may never get my shape back."

I pulled my hat over my eyes and tried to rest. I was beat. "Stop whining," I said. "We're making incredible time, and look at the Broken Sea. Isn't it beautiful?"

"What's your plan once we get on the island?" Zara asked as she tucked her arms under her head.

Oswald let out a shriek of laughter. "Plan?" he said. "Plan? Don't ask about plans. Jack and plans don't mix."

I pinched the homunculus hammock. He shrieked in pain. "Of course I have a plan," I said. "I always have a plan."

"You have plans. They just aren't any good."

"I have a simple and effective plan."

"Simple? They're all simple. Effective? Nope. Never."

"The best plans—"

"—are the simplest plans."

"I'm glad I taught you something, Oswald. The plan is to find the interdimensional baby before the Duke, destroy the Pandemonium Device, rescue the cats, and receive the reward."

"That's not a plan. That's a wish list. *How* are we supposed to find the baby before they do? Tell us that!"

"You're a stupid thing, Oswald. The baby will understand that we are there to help him and that the Duke is there to kill him. Therefore, he will make himself known to us and not them. It's so logical it's ridiculous. If the baby can't see that, he deserves to die."

"If the baby dies," Zara said, "we all die, genius."

"There's one or a million things wrong with that idea," Oswald said. "So, the baby is going to magically appear in front of us once we get to Monster Island? That's a bit too easy, don't you think? And maybe, if we ask the Duke to destroy the Pandemonium Device, he'll help us out?"

"Now you're being ridiculous, Oswald. There's no logic to that. Stop worrying. It'll work out. It always does."

"And I'm sure it will work out in harming me."

"Probably. But you're indestructible, so stop being a baby."

I listened to the beating of Camazotz's wings as we sliced through the Pandemonium sky. Black clouds scudded by and the stars burned as bright as dragon's eyes. Every now and then, Zotzy would dip or bolt upwards in his excitement, and I'd have to remind the bat god that he had passengers aboard. If we went crashing into the Broken Sea, we wouldn't have to worry about rescuing any demon baby. There was a sex-crazed shark woman below waiting to literally bang my brains out, and if she didn't get me, there was at least one kraken who'd take a stab at it.

Zara remained quiet for most of the trip, but then, out of nowhere, she said, "The Duke killed my father."

Maybe she was bored or just wanted to get it off her chest. I don't know.

"Your father?" I said.

"I'm pretty sure he did. Almost positive." She remained on her back with her hands under her head. She looked into the sky as she spoke. "I haven't told you guys everything. I met the Duke through my father. The Duke recruited him to build that stupid device. I didn't know at the time the wacko had no magical powers. Neither did my father. But it makes sense now. He needed him to handle the Jupiter Stone."

Camazotz slowed down at the mention of the Jupiter Stone. I feared he'd dump us into the ocean, but he kept on flying. I noticed he sped up quite a bit, though.

"I was so stupid," Zara said. "I had barely been out of Witch End, so I went along with my father to the palace. This was several years ago. And I fell in further and further with the Duke. I thought he was intriguing. What did I know?"

"He can be a real charmer," I said.

"No kidding. As my father spent every waking moment putting that machine together from the Duke's plans, I went off with the dirty liar. He wined and dined the hell out of me. But we knew nothing about the IDBs at the time. I don't know if my father would have cared either way. He wanted out of Pandemonium just as badly as the Duke. Maybe that's why I liked him. He reminded me of my dad."

"How did your father die?"

"In a freak accident with the device. Conveniently right after it was finished. The Duke said he had come into contact with the Jupiter Stone without protection, but my father was always careful. He had handled that stone for years without so much as getting a burn." I waited for Camazotz to say something, but he only huffed. "When I began snooping around and discovered the IDBs, that's when our relationship fell apart. When I tried to destroy the device, he locked me up."

"Why didn't he kill you?"

"First he tried to wipe my mind, then he tried to persuade me to join him. He promised to make me his queen or duchess or whatever when he gets to the Other World. But the Other World never held much interest for me. I was born here. I'm a Pandemonium gal."

"What about your mother?" Oswald asked. I thought it was an inappropriate question and was about to say so, but Zara said, "She's still alive, but she skipped out on us when I was still a baby."

"Was she really a pixie?"

"Yeah. Can you believe it?"

I said, "So your father was a normal-sized human? And your mother was a wee pixie?"

"I don't know how it worked," Zara said, "and I don't want to know. How were *you* made? Your mother fook a corpse?"

Oswald chortled. "I like her, Jack."

"Let's not talk about mothers, Oswald," I said. "For all we know, yours was a can of fluff."

"Come on, Jack, you know my parentage is a sore point."

"Same here," Zara said. "Mom didn't appreciate my non-pixieness and disowned me. If anyone tells me how cute and sweet pixies are, I'll scream. Last I heard, my mother was shacking up with a werewolf in the Red Garden."

Before things could get any more awkward, the mountains of Monster Island rose over the horizon. Jagged peaks pointed at the sky like the fingers of an arthritic giant. Shadows lurked among the obsidian rock, which reflected the red sky of Pandemonium. In the center of the island stood Pandemonium's tallest landform, Skull Mountain. A jumble of obsidian rock fifteen thousand feet high. Some say if you climb it, you can see the Other World from its peak. Others say you'll be eaten before you get ten feet off the ground. Sounds of night and hunger howled across the Broken Sea. If I wasn't already dead, I might have been terrified.

19

MONSTER ISLAND MASH

If the Broken Lands are Pandemonium's hell, Monster Island is its psych ward.

Wild and mountainous and shrouded in mystery, Monster Island was a no-man's land filled with Pandemonium's misfits, rejects, castoffs, and just plain weirdos. Chupacabras and cyclopes roam the hills, wendigos and bigfoots stalk the forests, sphinxes and gargoyles fly the skies, and headless horsemen and unicorns ride the roads. Then there are the monsters with no names. Them you don't want to run into.

I've had my suspicions that Oswald was born or created or spontaneously came into existence here. He's about as much of a reject as Pandemonium ever created.

Like most rational citizens of Pandemonium, I had never stepped foot on Monster Island. It wasn't a place you visited unless you had no choice or were looking for something. Like trouble.

Dark, frothing water crashed against the red-chalk cliff face at the shoreline. The Red Cliffs reached at least five hundred feet straight up.

The coastal area looked as if it was once home to a lush forest. But everything there was dead now. Ash and dust. Burnt tree stumps with gnarled, withered branches. Rock and deadfall. Nothing stirred on the ground. I should have been happy about that, but it only made me feel uneasy.

As we approached the island, I couldn't stop thinking about Ratzinger. The bastard was on Pandemonium somehow. And he had found me. I could feel him. I never minded being trapped in Pandemonium because I thought I was a dimension away from Ratzinger's corpse and the terrible things I had done in the Other World. But now the creep wasn't a corpse, at least not a dead one, and the horrors I thought were long buried had followed me here. Ukobach's words echoed in my head. "You are damned! Ratzinger is coming for you! Then you will know hell!"

Camazotz brought us down, none too gracefully, in a small clearing about a hundred yards from the cliff's edge.

Oswald immediately complained. "That was the worst hour of my life and I spent six months inside Jack's head."

"That wasn't a great six months for me either," I said and stretched my legs.

After a bit of doing, Oswald formed back into his annoying self. "Have you figured out how we're going to find this baby?"

The place gave me the creeps. The dead trees seemed to

lean towards us and thick, misshapen roots stuck up from the ground like the back of a crippled snake. The ground had a soft consistency, like sponge. It felt almost alive.

Camazotz still hadn't spoken. He'd been acting funny ever since Zara mentioned the Jupiter Stone. I thought maybe it had freaked him out. It certainly put a damper on his buzz. "Zotzy," I said, "I owe you some dust." I hoped that would cheer him up. Dust always cheers me up.

The bat god looked around and smiled.

"Can you guide us?" Zara asked.

He ignored her and said, "Keep the dust, Jack. I have what I wanted. I am home." And with that, he shot into the sky and disappeared.

"We just lost our ride," Zara said.

"But I just gained a baggie of dust," I said. I checked my pockets just in case Camazotz had stolen it. Thank Lucifer, it was all there.

"We could have used his help," Oswald said. "We're going up against an army of infernal creatures."

"You're such a woman, Oswald," I said, and Zara punched me in the arm.

"Remember, a woman saved both your arses," she said. "We should head toward Skull Mountain. It's the most likely place for them to set up shop. It's supposedly the closest you can get to the Other World. They may have been planning to kill the IDBs there the whole time."

I didn't like that idea. "We could be walking into a trap," I said.

"We've been on the island a whole five minutes," Oswald said, "and the baby hasn't appeared. Out of ideas, Jack?"

I was about to punt Oswald when I was proved wrong about the ground. It wasn't *almost* alive. It was most *definitely* alive. And it had decided we were for lunch.

Long, gray hands extended out from the roots and tree stumps and deadfall, wrapping around each of us. They dragged us along the ground toward a vast, exposed root system, where faces, ghostly and tormented, appeared along its surface. They stared out at us with desperate, wild eyes. But their faces weren't as terrifying as their screams and howls. A crying from deep inside the abyss. Full of despair and longing. And hunger. A terrible, insatiable hunger. Something even I couldn't fathom.

"Welcome to Monster Island," Zara said and then began thrashing at the branches that had wrapped around her legs and arms and throat. The haunted trees had a hard time holding onto Oswald, though. Every time they grabbed him, he either flattened himself or puffed himself up and broke their grip. I was wrapped up pretty tight, my arms pinned to my sides. I tried to bite the damn things, but I couldn't reach them.

"Anyone know what this thing is?" I yelled, fighting to keep the panic out of my voice.

"Hecatoncheires," Zara said. "If they pull us in, we'll join the other trapped souls."

Zara had freed one of her hands and went for her sledge-hammer, but a root smacked it away and three more wrapped around her.

"Oswald, stop messing around and do something!" I shouted.

I had sunk to my waist into the deadfall. I couldn't feel my legs.

Oswald was now eluding the reaching arms by bouncing like a ball. "I'm kinda busy here," he said.

I fell deeper into the haunted roots.

Zara closed her eyes as she mumbled to herself.

Did Camazotz know about this heca-whatever it was? And double-cross us? If I see him again I'm going to rip his new wings off.

Oswald bounded toward me. "Hurry, Oswald!"

The homunculus was too late. A hundred hands grabbed me from below and pulled me into the root system.

Though I heard the souls' cries outside, inside was perfect silence. And darkness. I swam in empty space, cut off from the world. Was this the absolute death?

A warm calmness filled me. I felt sleepy and at peace.

It didn't last long.

The darkness shrank and the souls of the damned surrounded me. With open mouths, they spun in a circle.

"Jack. You are so close now. I can almost smell your rot." That smooth, thick voice. Ratzinger. "We are going to be reunited soon, my son. Remember the fun we had in Krakow? You never ate so well."

I tried to curse the Nazi bastard, but no words left my mouth. I moved in the slow motion of a dream.

"Your soul will be mine again, and again you will lead my army. You were never much good at anything else."

The damned souls closed in, their mouths widening.

I shook in the dark void.

"Stupid Jack." Ratzinger laughed. "You don't have a soul. You have no place here."

The trapped spirits stopped spinning. Their mouths closed and then they began to shriek like banshees who lost their favorite toy. The darkness quaked and shimmered. I rose.

Light burned my eyes. I looked down. I was flying high above Monster Island. I caught a glimpse of Zara and Oswald looking up at me in disbelief. The roots lay limp on the ground around them. Apparently the heca-whatever had vomited me out and died. I guess it couldn't handle my soulless arse.

I soared over the wood like a clown shot out of a circus cannon and kept going until gravity remembered me. I tried flapping my wings but no dice. Zombies can't fly. Luckily, I fell into a river. Unluckily, it led to a waterfall.

I dropped fifty feet into raging rapids and took a little water ride. I came to a stop when a jagged boulder body-slammed me.

It was the second time in two days I had a traumatizing experience in water, but I still couldn't swim worth a damn. I doggy-paddled to shore, vowing to buy a life jacket as soon as I got back to ShadowShade.

A sharp pang of hunger tightened my guts. After my latest foray in hellish waters, not to mention Ratzinger's head games, I figured I was entitled to a hit of dust. I reached into my coat pocket. Crap on a stick! It was all gone. No dust. No hellfire sticks. This really wasn't my week.

20

INTERDIMENSIONAL BABY GOT BACK

I **had bigger problems than being dustless. I was lost** and had no idea where Oswald and Zara were. That probably didn't matter. The success of the mission was going to fall to me anyway.

Instead of looking for them, I set out to find the baby myself. How hard could it be on an island where everything was trying to eat me?

The forest was thick here, but fortunately I saw no exposed roots. I took a narrow path leading away from the river.

If I were an interdimensional baby, where would I go? What would I do if I were an itty-bitty interdimensional being with an attitude problem who was being hunted by two stupid leprechauns and a crazy human?

I'm a baby, so I would look for my interdimensional mama. No. He's not a baby. He's immortal, probably as old as or older than Pandemonium itself. Still, he'd look for something, a *proverbial* mama whose teat he could suckle after his ordeal with the heartless leps. Back to the womb, so to speak.

The leps are tracking him and bound him from leaving Pandemonium with some sort of magic. So...the baby would look for a way to unbind himself.

Where could he do that?

Where would the most powerful place on the island be? The nexus of power? The heart? The center? What's at the center?

Skull Mountain.

Didn't Zara say something about Skull Mountain? It didn't matter. She hadn't worked it out like me. She most likely took a blind guess.

I needed to find higher ground so I could triangulate the location of Skull Mountain.

Things—monsters I presumed—rustled in the underbrush and snarled. Every now and then something would bound through the bushes, unseen, snapping branches and making a racket. Then a three-headed dog loped across my path, no more than fifty yards ahead of me. It didn't even turn around. A second later I knew why. A hieracosphinx—a creature with the body of an enormous winged lion and the head of a hawk—broke out of the brush in pursuit. It, too, had no interest in me. Moments later, I heard a pitiful whelp followed by the wet lip-smacking of a carnivore eating *al fresco*.

I shambled a bit faster, my bones creaking worse than

ever. If this case didn't kill me, nothing would, and that was unfortunate.

Another hunger pang gripped me. If I ate the hieracosphinx, I could get whatever was left of the three-headed dog, too. No! I was going to close this case without eating anyone or anything. Then I thought of Fine Flanagan. Technically, though, that was *before* the case began so it didn't count.

Oswald would be proud, but then I thought how the little bugger always dismissed my plans and any nice feelings I had for him faded. Some people—especially homunculi—have no faith. And faith was all I had. I really had no idea how I'd find the baby. Winging it was my specialty.

I sniffed the air. I smelled the three-headed dog's blood. It was intoxicating. My usually dry-as-dirt mouth salivated. Something wailed. A baby? It come from my right, just off the path by a knot of trees. At least I hoped they were trees. Monster Island, I was fast learning, had a few tricks up its sleeve.

It was stupid, but I left the path and pushed through the brush. When I entered the clearing, I found myself a little surprise. It was giving me the finger.

The baby IDB!

I laughed and laughed and laughed. I nearly dropped to the ground. I pumped my fist.

"Fook you, Oswald! Fook you to high hell! Zombie one, homunculus zero."

To the baby, I said, "I knew we'd find you. It was logical. You know I'm your best chance to survive."

The cherub gave me the finger with both hands. He twisted

his chubby little fists and jabbed at the air like he was trying to pop a hole in it. He was really going to town with giving me the bird. "What's the deal? I'm here to save you, dunzy. Would you rather get caught by those stupid leprechauns?"

I crept toward the IDB. He didn't run away, which was good. I bent to pick up the little bundle of interdimensional joy, my back popping like bubble wrap. He vanished at the same moment I tripped the snare.

Whoosh! And I was hanging upside down ten feet above the ground.

Laughter. But not the good kind. They were clearly laughing *at* me.

"Smart zombie? Yeah, right."

"Fookin idiot, if you ask me."

Two leprechauns stepped out from behind a tree.

"We thought we'd never see ya rotten face again," the rat-faced one with the bigger shit-eating grin said. He wore a pointy forest-green hat at a jaunty angle. I wanted so bad to knock that damn hat off his head.

"The Duke told us you were in the palace, but he wouldn't let us pay you a visit. We had more urgent matters to attend to," the clurichaun said. He, too, wore a pointy hat, a red one, but it wasn't so jauntily worn. He was obviously the Beta Fairy.

"He assured us you'd die with the rest of Pandemonium. Me and Rory were so disappointed we didn't get a chance to murder ya filthy self."

"I figured out your plan and got here," I said. "Not so dumb after all."

"No, you're dumb," Rory said. "Don't you know zombies can't fly? We couldn't believe it when we saw you sailing through the air. We had a good laugh over that."

"And the Duke already has the last IDB and your friend, Zara Moonbeam. What was ya plan?" Jaunty said.

"It's classified," I said.

"Either way, in a half hour Pandemonium goes..." Jaunty made an explosion sound.

"Nice conjure with the baby, by the way. You fellas sure know your magic. How about letting me down?"

"Thanks. Liam"—that was the Jaunty One—"is working on his magic. He's not as good as Flanagan was."

"God rest his poor soul," Rory said and bowed his head.

"God rest his poor soul," Liam repeated and bowed his head, too. They had a moment of silence, which I broke. "Your pal is still with us," I said. "I never shat him out. Stick around, though, and maybe you can be reunited."

They both got as red as the clurichaun's overcoat.

"I know the Duke is in a rush," Liam said, "but we surely have time for some fun with this dirtbag."

Liam's shit-eating grin got a bunch shittier. He broke off a thick branch from a fallen tree, and Rory followed suit.

They worked me over as if I were a zombie piñata.

"Let's see if a zombie cries," one of them said. At that point, things got a bit blurry and confused.

One of the leps reared back and walloped me hard on the back.

All I kept thinking about was my poor suit. Forget a dry cleaning. I was going to need a elvish tailor.

They used my head like a tee. *Crack! Crack! Crack!* They broke my nose and set it back again, then broke it again. I never did cry of course, but they knew I wouldn't.

"This is for Flanagan!" *Whap!*

"This is for crashing into me car!" *Whap!*

"This is for being a dirty, rotten corpse!" *Whap!*

"This is for stinking like the fish market in Chinatown!" *Whap!*

"This is for being a soulless fook!" *Whap!*

I slipped into unconsciousness before they tired themselves out.

21

THE PANDEMONIUM DEVICE IS FULLY OPERATIONAL

When I awoke the first thing I saw was Zara Moonbeam.

"We have to stop meeting like this," I said.

"Do you remember who you are this time?"

"I'm the mayor of ShadowShade."

"Close enough."

We were lashed to metal posts set in the ground. From the looks of things, we were high up on Skull Mountain and had front-row seats to the Duke's cat massacre. About fifty yards in the distance, the infernal creatures had gathered around the glass jars containing the IDBs.

"Why didn't those leps kill me?" I asked.

"The Duke wants us to see his little show. The egotistical maniac spent a lot of time cooking up this plan and we're the only people outside of his lackeys who know about it."

"Always the showman."

The sky above Skull Mountain was the color of Lucifer's rotten heart. Bloated, black clouds rolled by. It looked like rain and hail were in the forecast.

"Where's Oswald?" I asked.

"He's under the mountain."

"That's where they buried him?"

"No. He's working on rescuing us."

"Oh, is he now?"

"I got caught on purpose. Isn't that what you did, too?"

I nodded. Maybe a bit too sharply.

"The rivers Mnemosyne and Lethe flow under the mountain," Zara said. "The plan is for Oswald to get the water of forgetting and drench the Duke and his minions. They'll forget their entire plan."

"And how exactly is he going to drench dozens of demons atop a mountain? Walk over to each and piss on them?"

"He wasn't sure about it. I'm hoping he'll figure it out."

"I'm sure he's brainstorming right now. We need to get off these posts."

The sky grew violent and hail began to fall. If the Duke didn't kill us, we'd probably get swept off the mountain. That was a comfort.

I watched as the evil fookers parted and the Duke passed between them. He headed toward us with the swagger of a man who had just been given the keys to the kingdom.

With two of his largest demons flanking him, the Duke stopped before us. "I'm terribly disappointed in you two." He shook his shiny, bald head in a dramatically slow way.

"I've been disappointing people since birth, pal," I said. "Get in line. By the way, your plan will never work."

"Not to brag, but I'm easily the smartest person in Pandemonium. It's not even close. So, I think I know a teensy bit more than a brainless zombie."

"Did you know your fly is open?" The Duke checked. It wasn't open. I don't even think he had a fly. "Outsmarted by a brainless zombie. Ha!"

The Duke gnashed his teeth. "The joke is on you, Jack. We're going back to the Other World and you're going to Hell, for real this time. But isn't that what you always wanted? See, we all win." He turned to Zara. "You're awfully quiet, my dear."

Zara rolled her eyes and turned away.

"I gave you a chance, Jack," the Duke said. "You are now just a spectator of the greatest show ever seen in Pandemonium. I hope you enjoy it. As for you, Zara, against my better judgment, I'll give you one more opportunity. Come with me. You can't imagine the life we will have together. A duke needs a duchess and I'd rather not see you destroyed along with the rabble."

Zara gave her answer in the form of a loogie, right in the Duke's eye. It slid down his cheek as he shook his head. He didn't bother to wipe it off. He turned and left with his two minions.

"You could have tried sweet talking him," I said when the Duke had returned to his staging area.

"I'm no good at it."

"You don't say?"

Straining and stretching my neck, I was able to make out the Pandemonium Device. It stood inside the circle of glass containers, a normal-looking black box about three feet high and six feet wide, except for Enochian forms etched on its surface. Thick, shiny black cables ran from the device into each of the vessels.

The Duke now stood in the circle next to the device.

The IDBs—including the baby—stood in their glass prisons, their heads slumped, their bodies slack.

"Loyal followers," the Duke said, in a voice loud enough for all of Pandemonium to hear. "Soon we will be free from this prison. Soon we will return to the Other World and take our rightful place as its masters. Too long have we rotted here. Too long have we been caged. Too long have we endured this nightmare dimension." I thought he was laying it on a bit too thick, but the demonic hordes ate it up. They howled and shouted and jeered in agreement.

I kept an eye out for Oswald, but I didn't have much hope. How could he possibly carry all that water up here and splash all these creatures without being seen? It was ludicrous. But that was the best they could come up with when I wasn't around. I almost blamed myself.

Each demon held a cat and a blade. I didn't know what would be worse: watching Pandemonium be destroyed or watching all those cats get butchered.

Hunger gripped me worse than ever. It felt like my insides

were twisting themselves into balloon animals. The shakes returned.

"Today we break the chains of oppression," the Duke said. "Today we go home." A thunderous roar exploded from the hordes. Hail rained down and pinged off the glass containers. When it hit the Pandemonium Device, the hail instantly disintegrated.

I took advantage of the shakes and shook and shimmied a bit more. I worked my left wrist hard against the ropes, trying to give myself the ol' Indian rug burn. Slowly, my skin peeled off. I kept at it as the Duke continued to pontificate about being oppressed and trapped in this terrible dimension and how awesome everything was going to be for them in the Other World. Darkness and ice cream every day.

I scraped and scraped my wrist against the rough rope until I created a groove. I gave my left hand a hard tug. I smelled burning flesh.

"What are you doing?" Zara asked.

"Trying to pull my hand off."

"Good thinking."

"By the way, aren't you a witch? Don't you know any rope-breaking spells?"

"Gee, why didn't I think of that? Abracadabra! Ropes, flee from my sight! Nope. Didn't work. Pull your fookin hand off!"

I gave it all I had and I yanked and yanked until I heard a snap. Then a twist and my hand fell to the ground. I had no problem then sliding the rope off and freeing my left hand.

"You can get that back on, right?" Zara asked.

"Oh, sure." It had been a while, though.

I swung my handless arm in front of me.

"What good is your arm without a hand?"

I nodded at the ground and Zara looked down as my hand crawled up my pant leg.

"Pretty creepy."

"Pretty useful."

"I won't ask about the other uses."

The hand crawled up to my other hand and quickly went to work on the rope.

"Nice going!" Zara said.

"Thanks. It really was nothing. Just the perks of being a re-animated corpse, I guess."

"I wasn't talking about you. Look!" She lifted her head to the sky.

I almost puked.

A hieracosphinx soared overhead and a very bloated Oswald sat atop its back. The little bastard!

At that moment, the Duke turned on the Pandemonium Device. It hummed to life with a deep rumbling that shook the ground. Bolts of lightning streaked across the insides of the glass containers and the IDBs writhed in pain.

"Hurry, Jack!" Zara said.

My severed hand was busily working on the rope, but it was knotted real good.

"I'm working on it."

Oswald looked like a giant weather balloon. I couldn't see his face, but I was sure he was smirking. Water shot out of his mouth like those fountains of naked babies and showered the demons at the edge of the circle. It wasn't long before they took to the air to intercept Oswald.

"Fook!" Zara shouted.

"What is it?"

"Oswald is using the wrong water. Look! It's white! That's the water of Mnemosyne!"

"That little idiot. I knew he'd screw this up."

I finally got my other hand free. I quickly untied my legs and then went to work freeing Zara.

All Oswald managed to do was piss off the infernal creatures, who didn't need much goading in that direction. More took to the sky to chase after him.

I caught a glimpse at the interdimensional beings. They were shrinking as the machine sucked the life out of them.

The hieracosphinx swooped and dodged the demons. Oswald continued to spit at them, but the water only made them stronger and faster as they gained abilities they had forgotten.

"Stop!" Zara was shouting. "It's the wrong water!" But Oswald was too far away to hear and having too much fun wetting the demons.

One demon broke from the pack and somersaulted headfirst into the hieracosphinx. All the water inside Oswald burst out and he went flying over the far side of the mountain. The hieracosphinx dropped straight to the ground. It tried to stand, but its legs were broken. A gaggle of demons pounced on it and tore it to shreds.

As I freed Zara, the hail fell harder and steam rose from the ground. The sky shimmered.

The Duke shouted and pointed at us. Three demons took off in our direction. I popped my hand back on.

"Now what?" Zara asked.

"We run."

We both took off in the opposite direction from the demons. I slipped and slid on the smooth-as-glass terrain. The hailstorm didn't help.

The hot, stinking breath of the demons tickled my neck. Their leathery wings cracked like shotguns blasts as they flew toward us. I ducked hailstones the size of orc fists and pulled my hat farther down on my head.

Zara stopped, turned, mumbled a few arcane words, and pulled the sledgehammer tattoo from her arm. She held up the iron hammer, reared back, and swatted a hailstone at the demons. It smacked the middle one right in the face. She swung again and hit another in the groin. The third demon tackled me.

We both went rolling down the mountain. I slammed into an outcropping at the mountain's edge and the demon slammed into me. He was on his feet first. The demon spread its wings and stomped toward me, smoke puffing out its nose and ears. Hailstones rained down on the creature, but it didn't seem to faze him. I picked one up and lobbed it at him. He swallowed the hailstone. Then he was on me. A taloned hand swatted me and I fell. The demon stood over me laughing. I slugged him on the jaw. He laughed harder. I got a real good look at his teeth. This guy obviously kept up his dental hygiene, because those were the whitest teeth I had ever seen. His breath wasn't so hot, though.

"You don't want to eat me," I said. "I'm spoiled."

His huge, knotted head lunged at me. Then, suddenly, he froze. His face twisted in agony. I thought he was having a heart attack, but it was much worse. The demon's abdomen bulged and tore open. Something emerged from his guts. Something black and lumpy. When it had made its way through, the black and lumpy thing looked up at me and said, "Hey, Jack, how's it going?" I screamed.

The head that had burst through the demon's stomach pulled back. The demon dropped to the ground and Camazotz stood before me, guts sliding off his face.

"You sure know how to make an entrance, Zotzy," I said.

Behind the bat god, a battle raged in the sky.

The Duke's minions were under attack from an army of Monster Island's finest: hieracosphinxes, giant bats, hawkmen, waspmen, pegasi, gargoyles, unicorns. Most of the others I had no name for. Giant bats tore demons in half and devoured them right there in the sky. Dragons spit fire at vampires, incinerating them.

Camazotz pulled me up. "I brought my friends," he said. "I thought you'd need the help."

"I thought you abandoned us."

"I'd never abandon a friend."

"Okay, pal. Let's finish this so I can get back home," I said, and we headed back toward the summit.

The top of Skull Mountain was anarchy. Demons battled in the air and on the ground. Blood and wings and limbs and guts flew everywhere. A hawkman came screaming out of the sky and dropped dead right at my feet.

The Pandemonium Device still hummed along. The IDBs were about half their original size now, their bodies contorting and shriveling in their glass vessels.

The sky rippled. The mountain rumbled and began to split apart. Tiny fissures sprouted along the ground.

"We need to find the Duke," I said, but Camazotz was gone. He liked doing that apparently. The guy must hate saying good-bye. I searched the sky and found him tearing apart a demon with his teeth.

I tried avoiding the battling monsters as I made my way toward the Pandemonium Device. The hum of the machine was deafening and the air around it was charged with static electricity. I didn't see the Duke or Zara.

I watched the baby IDB, his mouth stretched open in an agonizing scream. What made it more terrible was that I couldn't hear it. Lightning flashed inside the vessels, each strike twisting the interdimensional beings and reducing them.

The sky tore open like a sheet of paper, and there it was. The Other World. Clear as day. Even through the hail. I forgot all the colors. Bright sunlight peered through the thin veil between the two worlds. I must have been looking south, because I saw the Bronx and, beyond that, Manhattan. Giant buildings and trees. I had forgotten what green trees looked like. I didn't look at it too long because one of the leprechauns blindsided me. I went down like a bag of dirt.

As soon as I hit the ground, an earthquake seized the mountain. Rocks tumbled down, crashing into demons and Monster Islanders alike. A demon dropped out of the sky and landed right

on top of Rory the clurichaun. His stupid hat, not to mention Rory himself, was flattened like a pancake. Oh well. The other lep, Liam, looked at his fallen comrade, then at me. The sky flashed a brilliant red. The leprechaun with the jaunty-angled hat frantically searched the ground. I thought he was looking for a weapon, but he was after a cat.

The time must have come to exsanguinate the poor things.

One dashed across his path and the lep made a motion with his hand, obviously some kind of magic, and the cat slowed as if caught in molasses. Liam snatched the animal and held it up.

"You're a dead man!" the lep shouted at me.

"The joke is on you, buddy. I'm already a dead man."

As I've said, I'm not much of a sprinter. I'd never get to the lep in time. The cat was toast.

Then it hit me. I pulled off my left hand and chucked it. My hand tumbled finger over fist in the air and attached itself to Liam's throat. The lep dropped the cat and fell to the ground wrestling with my detached hand. I went to pounce on him, but between my pounce and my landing on the fairy, the ground shook and tore itself open. I landed inside a chasm. By the time I climbed out, the lep had managed to rip my hand from his throat.

He still had no interest in me, though. He only had eyes for the kitty cats. There was one cornered against a rock wall, and the lep crept slowly toward it.

I came up behind him. I swung at his head, but he ducked and spun around with a dagger in his hand. He punched it into my shoulder blade. I fell back. The lep went after the cat. I know I promised myself, but my hunger had reached its apex and this guy *really* deserved it. I sprang up and went into zombie mode.

Liam screamed bloody murder as I sunk my teeth into his calf, which I knew from experience was the tastiest part of the leprechaun. He was a bit gamier than Flanagan, but I'd still give him a rating of three shamrocks out of five.

I didn't get to finish, though. I had only just started on his guts when Zara screamed. It came from above.

I scrambled higher up the mountain, climbing on my hands and knees, until I got to the peak. There, I saw the Duke with Zara's sledgehammer and Zara on the ground bleeding from her mouth. The Duke looked even worse. His nose had been flattened and there was a dent the size of a sledgehammer head in his skull.

The Duke looked at me like I had walked in on him taking a leak. Zara tried to stand, but fell back to the ground.

"He distracted me, the weasel," she said, slurring her words. "Or I would have bashed in his fookin brains."

It looked like I had missed a hell of a fight.

"Give it up, Eddie," I said. "It's over. Without a cat, you're dead. Shut down the device and save yourself."

"Once the device is started it cannot be shut off," the Duke said. "I don't know about you two, but I'm going home." The Duke pulled out a cat from inside his tunic and grinned like a maniac. The cat mewled and tried desperately to get away from him.

I heard Zara mumbling to herself, but she was having a hard time getting the words out. At first, I thought she had lost her mind, but then I remembered that when the witch mumbled, some bad shit was about to happen. I just needed to keep the Duke talking.

"The cats won't save you," I said. "They don't have any magical qualities. You're fookin nuts, Eddie. You've always been nuts."

"I drank from Mnemosyne! I know shit! I know all kinds of shit you couldn't fookin imagine, corpse!"

Zara wiped dark blood from her chin. She raised her right hand and began to trace ancient figures in the air.

"I bet you're amazing at Twenty Questions," I said.

The Duke began to say something, but he gagged and heaved. He dropped the cat, which ran down the mountain. The gagging turned to full-on choking. Zara stood and walked toward the Duke, speaking that weird, lilting language. She took more blood from her face and described long, elegant shapes in the air. The Duke fell to his knees, his hands clawing at his throat. His eyes bulged, crazed with fear.

Zara stood over the lunatic. "This is for my father," she said and kicked him over the edge of the mountain. I listened as a long, bloodcurdling scream faded into silence.

She grabbed her sledgehammer and returned it to her arm.

"We need to find Oswald!" I said.

We headed down the other side of the mountain, in the direction the little guy went flying. By now, most of the demons had been killed. Their bodies piled high on the mountain. We climbed over heaps of demon carcasses on our way and, a few times, had to duck as more bodies fell out of the sky.

"Oswald!" Zara shouted. "Oswald!"

The hum of the Pandemonium Device grew louder as the sky grew brighter. I could see white, puffy clouds and the sun now.

I'm so attuned to Oswald's stupid little voice that even over the din I heard a little pip. I followed it and spotted his legs peeking out from under a pile of fallen rocks. "Zara, over here!"

I pulled on his legs, but I couldn't move him.

Zara ran over, took a look, and smeared her fingers with the blood dripping from her head. She drew a sign on the rocks and they turned to dust. We lifted Oswald. He looked pretty beat, but he opened his eyes. "Jack, did we stop the demons?"

"Sort of." I'd wait to tell him how royally he screwed up. But now he had a chance to make up for it.

We ducked and dived past falling demons and hail and rock slides until we made it back to the device. The IDBs were nearly gone, only their essences remained in the containers, tiny balls of intense light. Bursts of lightning bounced off the orbs. Below, the skylines of Manhattan and the Bronx flickered in and out. The mountain swayed like a drunken ghost pirate. There wasn't much time. I thought about grabbing a cat. But just for a second.

"Okay, I have a plan," I said.

I stood Oswald on the ground. He wobbled a bit but remained upright. "I already have a problem with that," he said.

"This is going to work."

"How is this going to hurt me?"

"If we don't do this, we're all going to be hurt real bad."

"What's the plan?"

"We can't turn off the device."

"We're running out of time," Zara said.

The world shook and we all fell.

After struggling back up, I said, "Oswald, seeing as though you're indestructible, you need to cover the device, and Zara here is going to smash it with her sledgehammer."

"And what are you going to do?"

"I'm going to applaud you for saving the world. Isn't that what you've always wanted?"

"I want to be a full partner in the agency."

"Now wait a minute! Don't go strong-arming me!"

"He's a fookin full partner!" Zara said. "Stop wasting time!"

The device hummed like a billion wasps in a maelstrom. The orbs inside the vessels dimmed.

I didn't have the energy to fight Oswald or Zara. "Fine," I said. "Whatever you want."

"I want my name on the business cards and on the office door."

I was about to say something, but Zara smacked me in the ear. "Oswald, buddy, get in there and make us proud."

"You called me your *buddy*."

"I might have misspoken."

Oswald's grin was so wide that his head looked like it was about to split open. "I don't believe everything they say about zombies, Jack." Oswald winked, jumped into the circle, and spread himself out into a long, flat sheet. He then flung himself over the device. Zara uttered her magical words, touched her sledgehammer tattoo, and pulled out the weapon. She held it at the ready.

"Are you sure this will work?" she asked.

I shrugged. "Fifty-fifty chance?"

Zara grimaced and swung her hammer down on the center of Oswald. At once, two things happened: the world went silent as if all the air had been sucked out of Pandemonium, and a burst of brilliant white light exploded from underneath Oswald.

Skull Mountain jumped and rattled. Rocks showered down on us and the ground tore open.

I didn't remember falling, but next thing I knew I was on my back, looking up at the sky as the blue bled away to red.

I grabbed onto the edge of a thin fissure and closed my eyes. I was sure we'd all get swept off the mountain, but then, as quickly as it all happened, it stopped.

The fat, black clouds returned. The hail, thankfully, did not.

I struggled to my feet.

Zara sat on a rock, shaking her head. Oswald was still stretched out like a sheet in the middle of the IDBs. I rushed over to him and got on my knees. "Oz," I said, shaking him, "you can get up now." He didn't move. His body was limp and unresponsive.

I peeled him off the ground, revealing a crater that seemed to reach to the bottom of Skull Mountain. The device was gone. Most likely it had been obliterated along with the Jupiter Stone. And poor little Oswald swallowed the impact.

I draped him over a boulder, but he just lay there like a bedsheet. I knelt beside him and rubbed and kneaded him like a lump of dough.

"Stop screwing around, Oswald," I said.

"He's indestructible, right?" Zara asked. She stood beside me, rubbing her jaw.

"That has always been my belief."

In the middle of the sheet that was now Oswald were two faint X's. I remembered scratching them into his head. Living things, I had said to him at the time, need eyes. Otherwise, it's creepy as fook.

"Your belief?" Zara said.

"He's always come out okay before."

"That was before he took on a Jupiter Stone."

"Oswald, if you're playing games, you're out of the agency! This isn't funny anymore." I really needed a Lucky Dragon.

"Are you crying?"

"It's sweat."

"Coming out of your eyes?"

I turned toward the containers and wiped my sweaty eyes. The IDBs were all glaring at us, particularly the cherubic one.

"I think they want to be let out," Zara said.

The interdimensional beings had returned to their humanoid forms but still looked to be in bad shape. Their ribs were visible through their now thin and gray skin.

"You're the one with the sledgehammer," I said.

Zara walked over to the first container and smashed it. The silver-eyed IDB breathed the air and, in a blink, disappeared. No thanks, no nothing. Zara went around the circle, smashing the containers. The last was the baby's. I stood and we looked at each other for a moment after Zara broke him out. He looked at the crater where the device had been. He nodded at me, and then he gave me the finger and flew off. Maybe that was how they thanked people. Or maybe he was the most ungrateful creature in the universe. I kind of admired his spunk, though.

I continued to rub and knead Oswald as Camazotz swooped down from the sky and landed beside me.

"The battle has ended," he said. "We were victorious."

"Good going, Zotzy," I said.

"Was that your friend?" Camazotz asked, looking down at Oswald.

I didn't know what to say, so I said nothing. I tried squishing Oswald into a ball, hoping I could reshape him.

I was bouncing him on the ground when the sky blackened and blacker creatures appeared. They circled the mounds of fallen monsters and demons. Their long, thin wings flapped in half-time. Their beaks were like ice picks. They had no eyes.

Strands of light rose from the dead and the creatures swallowed them.

"What the hell are those things?" Zara asked.

"Soul Suckers," Camazotz answered.

A chill flew up my spine. These things had Ratzinger's stench all over them. He was already gathering his army.

The winged nightmares made lazy circles as they sucked up the demonic souls and inched toward us.

"We have to go," I said.

I put Oswald in my pocket and gave him a pat.

As I was about to head down the mountain, a gang of black cats surrounded me. I had forgotten about the kitties. I didn't count them, but I was pretty sure it was fifty-two. I took a couple of steps forward and they followed.

"See, they found me because they know I'm here to save them," I said. "It's logical."

Zara walked over to me and sniffed my suit. "That's not it, you stupid corpse. You reek of kraken and the Broken Sea. These poor cats must be starving."

Several of them licked my shoes and pants.

The Soul Suckers squawked.

"Jump on my back, Jack," Camazotz said, "and I'll fly you out of here."

"I need to get these cats back to the goblin queen or no more dust."

Camazotz whistled and his comrades appeared. He explained the situation and each one took a cat. Zara hopped on the back of a pegasus.

"I'm not going back to the Broken Lands," she said. "I think I'll visit the Red Garden. Maybe Mother will be happy to see me this time."

"If you ever need a P.I., here's my card," I said. I pulled out a very dirty and tattered business card and handed it to her. "I'll give you a good discount."

She took it, placed it against her left inner forearm, and it turned into a tattoo.

Camazotz whistled again and we all shot into the Pandemonium sky.

22

FEAR AND LOATHING
IN SHADOWSHADE

The dust was nearly all gone. Seven fookin kilos. Right up my nose. I think I had burned another hole in my nostrils. I swear I could hear pixie wings fluttering in Fairy Land and vampire fangs extending on Blood Beach and were-wolf hair growing in Werewolf End. This must have been what the Duke felt like after he drank all that memory juice. Except I felt like crap. Sweat covered my body in a thick sheen. My hands shook and my throat was dry as troll skin.

I flattened myself against the office wall, carefully pulled open a tiny fraction of the blinds, and took a quick glance out the window. The creep in black was still there, standing on the corner across the street. Five hours now. He looked up at my office, and I pulled my hand back. I slid away from the window and

opened my top desk drawer. There was maybe a one-week sup-
ply of dust left, if I stretched it out.

The goblin queen had been generous. When I arrived in Goblin Town with all of her cats, she was ecstatic. She couldn't
thank me enough. I don't think she believed I'd find them. She
kept throwing dust at me. When I filled my pockets, she shoved
more dust in my hands. I needed a chest to carry it back to
ShadowShade. I think I'm an honorary goblin now. She even
hooked up Camazotz and his pals. We partied for three days in
Goblin Town before we got straight enough to leave. Camazotz
ditched me again. I barely remember how I got home. I think
I hitched a ride with some merfolk. I sure hope it wasn't that
crazy shark woman.

Oswald still hadn't woken up. I asked the goblin queen if she
could help, but she didn't even know what Oswald was. Camazotz
had no clue either. Oswald is a damn riddle wrapped in a mystery
inside a marshmallow. I wasn't sure if he'd ever wake up.

I sat and stared at the white blob, which now sat on my desk.
He had kept rolling off, so I secured him between an empty bottle of Devil Boy and my orc skull ashtray. The runt didn't even
make a decent paperweight.

When I got back to ShadowShade I locked myself up in my
office and went to town with the dust. Without Oswald to stop
me, I went off the rails. I felt empty inside, like I was missing
something vital. It wasn't because of Oswald! But, boy, did I feel
bummed. Maybe it was because I had saved the damn world
and no one knew. The newspapers didn't want to hear from me.
I was still a broke, undead bum.

I peeked out the window again. The creep in black still stood on the corner, a folded-up newspaper under his arm. He was an agent of the mad Nazi doctor, I was sure of it. The dust didn't help with my growing paranoia surrounding Ratzinger, but it wasn't paranoia. The fook was really out to get me.

Every night since I had returned, I dreamed of Ratzinger. His voice burning in my brain. "Jackie boy, I'm coming to get you. Jackie, I'm close to finding your soul. Jackie, you're going to make a great general for the dead." The dust was the only thing that silenced the voice.

I reached for a bottle of Devil Boy in the bottom drawer, but it was empty. I buzzed the intercom. "Lilith," I said, "do we have any more formaldehyde?"

The ghost drifted through the wall. Lilith wore a flowing white gown, tiara, and pearl necklace. Her hair was made up in an impossibly tall beehive. She was ready for the ball to end all balls. She had been ready for three centuries, actually, but she never made it. She died when her carriage was besieged by highwaymen.

"Lilith, what did I say about going through the walls? Use the damn door, please. This is a professional joint." Lilith has her quirks, but she works for free so I really can't complain. Not that I had much choice in the matter. She had been haunting my building for decades. I gave her a job to make her useful.

"Sorry. Next time. We're all out of formaldehyde. You've been drinking up a storm since Oswald died."

"Oswald's not dead!" I shouted. I think spit shot out of my mouth. Maybe my nose, too.

"Sure, sure. He's just sleeping, Jack."

"What do you know, Lilith? Oswald isn't like the rest of us."

"Do you want me to try calling Wally the Wizard again? He might be able to help. I think he's back from Purgatory Island."

"What did they pinch him for this time?"

"I think he was selling fake philosopher stones."

"Forget that guy. He's a charlatan. We need someone big. A sorcerer supreme or a mad scientist or maybe a god. Did you ever hear back from Lucky McGuire?"

"No word. He's lying low after the leprechaun queen put a hit out on him."

"Great. He's the best snitch in town, but he'll never surface if Dana is after him. Find me a god. Greek, Norse, Hindi. I don't care."

"I'll get on it."

"Get the Devil Boy first."

"Sure thing, boss."

Lilith floated through the wall. From behind, she wasn't so glamorous. The back of her head was bashed in and pieces of brain oozed out. That was the highwaymen's handiwork. They used a hammer. "Door!" I shouted as she disappeared into the reception area. Ghosts! So set in their ways.

I lifted Oswald. He seemed just a ball of fluff, but the little bugger was heavy as hell. In fact, he seemed like he had gained some weight. Dead weight, I guess. Could Oswald really be gone? The weirdo was just rubber and marshmallow. He had no heart or brain or internal organs. I bounced him in my hand. Did he have a soul? And now he doesn't? Did the Jupiter Stone destroy it? Did Ratzinger's Soul Suckers take it? What the hell is a soul anyway? I've gotten along without one for decades and I'm fine. Well, fine-ish.

His X eyes were the only things that showed he was him. I waved my hand before them, trying to get a reaction.

I'm not proud to admit it, but I had shoved the homunculus back into my skull, hoping that would revive him. I kept him in there for five days, but nada. I just got a splitting headache.

When he returns, I'm going to give him such hell.

I put Oswald back on the desk, gave him a little pat.

The intercom buzzed. Lilith squawked, "There's someone here to see you, Jack."

"Send them away," I said.

I had turned down three jobs since I returned. One was for a missing hunchback grandpa from Vodun Heights, another was a surveillance job on an unfaithful werewolf, and the third was a vampire looking for his long-lost love, most likely so he could drain her of her vital essence. And I needed the money, too. Just as I thought, my suit needed extensive dry cleaning and tailoring and my fedora needed blocking. (I passed on deodorizing it all. I've gotten used to my odor.) I didn't have the heart to take the cases, though. No, it had nothing to do with Oswald! I'm perfectly capable of solving cases without him. I just needed a break. Saving the world takes a lot out of a person.

"He insists," Lilith said. "He says it has to do with your missing soul. He says you'd know what's at stake."

I broke out in another sweat. If I had a heart it would have been trying to break out of my chest right now. I reached for the bottle of Devil Boy, then remembered it was empty. Fook! I took a quick hit of fairy dust, gave myself a couple slaps to the face, and said, in a controlled voice, "Send him in, Lilith."

The door opened and—wouldn't you know it?—it was the creep in black. Paranoia my arse. I was back in business. But business wasn't good.

DEAD JACK: BOOK 2 COMING SOON!

A DEAD JACK SHORT STORY

THE CASE OF THE
AMOROUS OGRE

GWENDOLYN

She was thirty-two inches of nauseating cuteness in an itty-bitty emerald dress that made her seem, somehow, more naked than if she wore nothing at all. Her skin was snowflake white, her hair torchlight red, her eyes tiny blue moons. And if I wasn't such a smart guy I'd have thought she was a child. But she was probably five centuries past her sweet sixteen. The little lady sat across from my desk, her thin, see-through wings twittering nervously.

She said her name was Gwendolyn. She was a pixie.

I poured myself a shot of Devil Boy. "Care for some?" I said. "Looks like you might need it."

She pulled on one of her pointy ears. "I don't drink formaldehyde."

Lilith, my secretary and the resident office ghost, told me the pixie was in trouble. Of course she was in trouble. Why else would she be in the same room as a zombie?

I threw back the formaldehyde, most of which poured out from the bottom of my skull. The pixie's face scrunched up in disgust.

"Gwen, let me ask you something. Any of you pixies not so goddam adorable?" It wasn't a compliment.

She tugged down on her flimsy get-up. She covered an extra inch of thigh, but also managed to expose a healthy chunk of pixie cleavage. If I wasn't a zombie, I'd be sweating buckets now.

"Can we, please, get down to business?" she said. "I was told you're the best detective in Pandemonium. Was that a lie?"

I don't know who told her that, but I should hire him to do my PR. I wasn't the best, just the cheapest. Which is why I got the dirtiest cases in the Five Cities.

"Gwen, everyone lies in this business, but you got the rare truth." I threw back another shot of Devil Boy.

"Then you should have no problem rescuing my daughter."

"I rescue daughters all the time. It's one of my specialties." Actually I never even rescued a gremlin from a tree. But, as I said, everyone lies in this business.

Finally the pixie got into it. "My daughter, Willa, she's a very naïve girl. But that's to be expected: she's only two hundred and twelve years old. And if you know anything about pixies, especially young ones, they're always getting into mischief. It's usually harmless pranks: stealing horses, leading people astray, that sort of thing. But lately she's been getting into real trouble. Running with a bad crowd, going places a pixie shouldn't go. I forbid her to go uptown. There are bad types there—"

"Ogres."

"Yes, ogres. And one of those vile, disgusting beasts has taken a fancy to my Willa. I believe his name is Mad Dog."

"Madgogg?"

"Yes. You know him?"

"Heard of him. I told you I'm the best. In fact, I already know why you're here: Madgogg abducted your daughter, is holding her in his ogre lair, and demands that she marry him, right?"

"Yes, yes, it's horrible."

"It's an old story, Gwen. Happens every day."

"An ogre in the family! I'd never stand for it."

"Ogres are stupid, predictable creatures. I've dealt with a few in my time. No worries."

I didn't mention that ogres also like to eat pixies, but she probably already knew that. I also didn't mention that zombies like to eat pixies, too, and just about anything else with succulent, sweet, so juicy flesh. But I kicked that habit (mostly) long ago. I said, "I just need one kilo of fairy dust a day plus expenses." I didn't tell her how badly I needed the dust. It had been a while since my last fix and I was getting hungry.

A SIMPLE PLAN

Black, tentacled clouds drifted across the blood-red sky as I drove toward the Upper West Side of ShadowShade. The forecast called for more dry heat with a chance of firestones. Creepy shit. But par for the course in Pandemonium, the twilight realm of nightmare creatures, legends, the undead, and everything in between. Home shitty home.

ShadowShade was actually the more cosmopolitan and sophisticated of Pandemonium's Five Cities. It has streets and a subway (though you don't want to go down there if you're afraid of eyeless mole people), unlike those other Podunks.

I watched blood-drunk vampires stumbling out of the Full Moon Saloon, the most notorious watering hole in Hell's Kitchen, and werewolves playing patty-cake with virginal waifs at the edge of the Wood of Shadows.

Madgogg had a brownstone on West 93rd that overlooked the Wood. It was a high-rent area for the well-to-do ogre, and many ogres were well-to-do these days. Droves of the brutes were leaving their cramped huts in Ogreville, nestled in the eastern corner of the Broken Lands, and buying up ShadowShade's most expensive real estate. Their success must have something to do with their big bodies and little brains.

My plan, like all my plans, was simple:

1. Disguise myself.
2. Infiltrate Madgogg's brownstone.
3. Rescue the captive pixie.

In and out. Easy-peasy.

I parked around the corner from Madgogg's place, on West 92nd, nearly running over a careless succubus who was walking her pet midget dragon. As I walked toward the brownstone, I was having second thoughts about the disguise. The hump was biting into my back and the wig was itching like mad. The itching made me wonder where Oswald was. I hadn't seen him in a while. And that worried me.

I knocked at the servant's entrance on the ground floor of Madgogg's brownstone, and a few minutes later an ancient-looking zombie opened the door. He must have spent a long century dead before being reanimated, which was good—because his brains would be mush and the dummy would be a pushover.

"Hey there, bones," I said.

The dummy stared at me, his lifeless eyes wide and protruding from their sockets. He was a skeleton in a suit. Most likely imported from the Zombie Islands to be a domestic. These guys made me sick.

I said, "I'm the new hunchback handyman." I pointed to the hump for emphasis. "The agency sent me over."

The creature stood there silently, his exposed jaw hanging open. I wasn't so sure if he was reanimated after all. Then he nodded and let me in.

The kitchen was huge. The cauldron in the middle of the room was huge. The three-headed dog inside the cauldron was pretty huge, too. The middle head looked particularly nasty, but none of them were gonna do me any harm. They were ogre lunch. It stunk worse than a zombie's armpit in there.

I walked through the kitchen and entered a long hallway paneled with the heads of trolls, gremlins, and at least one goblin. There weren't any zombie heads, so I stupidly felt safe. But then I figured zombie heads probably aren't worth much as trophies.

I heard a series of low moans coming from behind the door at the end of the hall. The door was unlocked. I opened it.

It was the door to the basement. Nothing good is ever in the basement, so naturally I went down.

At the bottom of the staircase, the moans were clearer. I heard some grunts, too.

Another door stood before me, iron and heavy and unlocked, too. This Madgogg must be a real dunzy or real confident. The plan was working to perfection. I could already taste the fairy dust on my desiccated lips. I could also taste flesh and blood and brains—and without that fairy dust to kill the cravings, I was liable to eat half of ShadowShade. And most likely get a stake through the head, too.

I entered a long, brightly lit hall. On the right was a rough stone wall, and farther up on the left was a prison cell.

The moaning sounds were coming from inside the cell and

now I could make out what they were. Someone was eating and they were enjoying it! I felt a pang of jealousy, but I curbed the zombie in me and rushed down the hall. I had to kick aside garbage that littered the floor—wrappers, empty containers, dirty plates. Ogres had mighty appetites, but this looked bad.

I stopped before the heavy iron bars of the cell. I couldn't believe my bloodshot eyes. Fancy tapestries hung on the walls. A gigantic bed with a silk canopy took up almost half the room. And in the middle of the chamber, on a chaise lounge, sat a plump, short girl with wings. They fluttered like mad. Her mouth was fluttering like mad, too, as it tore through a turkey leg. The moaning was coming from her. Obviously she liked to eat.

She looked up, took another bite of the turkey leg, swallowed, and then said, "Jeez, another hunchback handyman. Don't you guys ever do anything else?"

"Are you Willa?"

She picked a piece of turkey not quite the size of my fist out of her teeth and said, "What's it to ya?"

She resembled her mother, if Gwen had a serious food addiction. I finally had an answer to my question: Yes, there are pixies who are not so goddamn cute.

"I'm here to rescue you," I said.

Her eyes widened and then she screamed, "What the hell is coming out of your nose?!"

I panicked for a split second. As a member of the undead, I often find myself in embarrassing social situations, such as when worms exit my body during interrogations or body parts fall off at dinner parties. Unsurprisingly I don't find myself on many guest lists. Then I felt a tickle in my nose cavity and I relaxed. But just a bit.

"That's just my associate," I said.

Oswald's soft, gelatinous body oozed out of my right nostril. It wasn't an unpleasant sensation; probably the only thing that wasn't unpleasant about Oswald. He dropped onto the floor with a heavy plop and instantly began to transform, tightening and twisting into the shape of a tiny man.

"Oswald, where the blazes have you been?"

He didn't answer right away. He was busy inching toward a potato chip under the chaise lounge.

"I thought you were mad at me," the homunculus said.

"I *am* mad at you. I'm always mad at you."

"What the hell kind of hunchback are you?" Willa said.

I leaned closer to the bars and whispered, "I'm not really a hunchback. I'm a detective. A zombie private eye, in fact. And let's keep it down. We don't want to arouse the ogre while we're trying to rescue you."

"You don't think Reginald will let you walk right out the door with me, do you?" Willa said.

"Listen, we need to get you out of here. Reginald—who the hell is Reginald?"

Willa pointed over my left shoulder.

"He's the ogre standing behind you."

"Wonderful," I said, and then experienced the closest thing to sleep possible for a zombie.

PLAN B

Zombies don't usually get headaches. So the throbbing in my skull must have been a delusion. I was praying that the straps across my chest and legs were a delusion, too, but I didn't have much luck convincing myself.

Thick leather belts held me to a steel table, not unlike those slabs on which corpses rest in the morgue. As if I'd know anything about that.

The room was cozy, if you happened to be a ghoul. To my right, surgical tools were neatly laid on a long, low table. A shelf above that held various bottles and jars containing glass eyes, ceramic horns, and various other fake body parts. Stuffing lay in heaps in the far corners of the room. Another table, directly in front of me, held a padlocked wooden box and more stuffing. To my left, next to the window, hung a plaque from one of those correspondence courses, certifying one Reginald Belial Madgogg for taxidermy. So the big oaf has a middle name, too.

Something tickled my right ear.

Then I heard a little whiny voice. "That was your brilliant plan, huh? Just waltz in, grab the pixie, and waltz out?"

I couldn't see Oswald's face, but I was sure he had that condescending look he always gets: head cocked to the side, eyes rolled up, lips pressed together. The best way to describe Oswald? Imagine a marshmallow with a mouth and X's for eyes. I had to scratch those eyes in. If you can speak, you should have eyes. Otherwise, it's damn creepy.

"The best plans, Oswald, are the simplest ones," I said.

"Well, my dead friend, do you have a Plan B?"

"I'm thinking."

Oswald hopped onto my chest. He stared at me. Now, he was wearing his I-know-something-you-don't expression. If Oswald had pants, he'd be wetting them.

"Well, don't strain your worm-eaten brain thinking anymore. I learned something very interesting after that ogre clobbered you and you fell like a sack of dead kittens."

"He surprised me! How was I supposed to know there was a hidden door behind me?"

"Anyway, I hid in the cell after transforming myself into a puddle of goo. And after stowing you away in here, Madgogg came back and, boy oh boy, what a smooth-talker this guy is. He's sweet-talking our pixie, promising her everything under the moon: jewels, midget dragons, silks, those golden fish that grant you wishes. Then get this—he promises her his soul. But he means it, literally. He tells her his soul isn't in his body. It's hidden on some place called Black Rock, which is suspended over the Undead Sea."

"Of course!" I said. "It's an old ogre trick. They remove their souls from their bodies, because it somehow makes them invulnerable, and they hide the soul in some hard-to-reach place. Oswald, I get that soul, I hold all the cards. Either he gives me Willa or I crush his soul. It's the perfect plan."

Oswald was starting to get bent out of shape, literally. His gelatinous body bulged and warped, going in and out from little man shape to blob shape. That was a bad sign.

"There are a few problems, Jack." It was even worse when he called me Jack.

"Problems are my business."

"First of all, the soul is inside an egg..."

"Okay."

"...which is inside a box..."

"Big deal."

"...which is inside a goose..."

"I can deal with a goose."

"...which is inside a jackal."

"Okay, so there are some livestock issues."

"That's the least of the issues. The jackal is protected by five demons."

"So what? Oswald, scoot up to this Black Rock, retrieve the soul, and get back here pronto. I'll handle the rest."

"Me? You want *me* to get the soul? I can just untie you and we'll go—"

"There's no time! Go immediately!"

"You're still afraid of the water, aren't you?"

"Listen, you little freak, I'm not afraid of anything. There's simply no time."

"I'll just untie you—"

"If you don't leave this instant, you are out of the agency!"

"How am I even supposed to find this stupid rock?"

"How many rocks can be suspended over the Undead Sea? Ask around, dunzy."

THE SOULMAN COMETH

Afraid of the water? I might not have minded that from anyone else. But from a homunculus?

Who wouldn't be afraid of the water after having been trapped in it for a week? One of the many disadvantages to being a zombie is that you can't die—and that was one time when I would have welcomed it. Zombies and sailing do not mix.

I was beginning to look fondly on that time. The damn wig was itching worse than the maggots on Corpse Hill, the hump was digging into my back like a drunken succubus, and my hunger was growing. I fantasized about thick waitress thighs and fat lawyer bellies and grad-student brains. I know it's a nasty habit, but I've been able to control it, mostly. Of course, most zombies aren't known for their control. So I guess I'm not your typical zombie.

Through the window at my left, I could see the firestones pouring from the crimson sky. The weatherghoul was right again! The demons would be out now. They always come out during inclement weather, blackening the skies over Shadow-Shade, swooping and dipping and snatching a lonely fairy or unicorn.

Then I saw Oswald's head coming over the windowsill. He was smiling like a lunatic gnome. I didn't know what was worse: Oswald failing, or Oswald succeeding and rubbing it in my face.

He hopped into the room. He was dragging a large sack behind him.

"I got it," he said. His body glowed with an internal devil's fire.

I shouted, "What the blazes took so long? It must have taken you at least *four and a half* hours!"

"For your information, there were *three* rocks suspended over the Dead Sea, which, I should remind you, isn't just a hop, skip, and jump away. And did you forget the five demons?" He glowed brighter. "It was pretty rad, actually. Let me tell you how I vanquished them—"

"Put it in your report. Now hurry and untie me."

"Couldn't I have done that before?"

I glared at the runt. Homunculi don't know the first thing about respect. That's why they're little men. "Okay, okay," he said and jumped onto the table, where he began to cut the straps with a scalpel.

"So, anyway, I used a feather slathered with peanut butter—"

"Peanut butter? If you used the petty cash to buy yourself food, I'm taking it out of your salary. Now stop wasting time! File a report and maybe I'll read it. But proofread the damn thing this time and don't embellish."

The sack glided across the floor.

"Oswald?"

"Yeah?"

"Why is the soul gliding across the floor?"

"There was a bit of a problem."

"There's always a problem with you!"

The homunculus finally freed me. I sat up. I was so stiff I thought my rigor mortis was acting up again. I stood and stretched. I think I heard a vertebra snap. Then I ripped off the wig and hump. I felt better then, except for the gnawing at my rotten innards. The hunger was reaching critical mass. All I could think about was fairy dust. I reached for my Lucky Dragon hellfire sticks, but they were gone. The ogre must have stolen them!

The sack was now banging against the wall.

"Let me show you the problem," Oswald said and hopped down from the table. He ran over to the sack and untied the string that held it shut. Out tumbled a small, and terribly confused, white goose.

"I was able to make the jackal puke up the goose," Oswald said. "But it won't work on the goose. He won't give up the box!"

I picked up the creature and knocked on its stomach. I heard a dull thud. Indeed, the box was there.

"Do you have any ideas?" Oswald said.

"Yes, of course I do!" I said and sunk my teeth into the goose. It squawked twice, perhaps three times, and then went silent. I tore through the creature, swallowing feathers and flesh. It was electric, life coursing through me and warming me. I felt like a phoenix burning back into existence. If Oswald hadn't stopped me, I'd have eaten the box, too.

"What has gotten into you?" Oswald shouted. "I thought you were done with that! We don't need another episode."

I dropped the goose carcass, wiped the blood from my mouth. Already the rush was draining from my black veins. "I need that fairy dust, Oswald. I'm on the verge of eating all of Shadow-Shade and maybe even parts of the Red Garden."

"Just hold it together. We'll get the damn dust."

I held up the box. It barely weighed a thing. But before I could ponder the insubstantial nature of souls, I heard a deep-throated grunt.

The ogre stood in the doorway.

Madgogg had to duck to get inside the room. He was green as

a goblin, bald, and uglier than a vampire exposed to the sun. A gold earring dangled from one of his sharp, bat-like ears.

"Just the man I wanted to see," I said.

The ugly sucker was trying to look mean—and doing a damn good job of it. Thank goodness I had this guy's soul in my hand or I might have been petrified.

"Listen, you overgrown gnome," I said, flipping open the box. Inside, nestled in velvet, sat a small white egg. "The dance is over. You've been outsmarted." I held up the egg between my thumb and forefinger. "Madgogg, I hold here an egg—a very special egg—that I took great pains to retrieve."

In my mind, I felt Oswald's eyes roll.

The ogre remained silent, but he huffed and his face burned a bruised red.

"It's gonna go like this, Reg," I said. "You're gonna give up this obsession of marrying a pixie—which, quite frankly, is pathetic. You're gonna give up the girl and we're all gonna march out of here unharmed."

The ogre lumbered toward me.

"Let Willa go and I'll return your soul," I said. "Fair trade."

I backed up, but just a dozen steps.

The ogre kept lumbering.

"I happen to know that if I destroy this egg, you're finished. Walk another step and I'll make myself an ogre omelet."

The ogre walked another step. In fact, he walked quite a few steps.

I gave the dunzy ample warning. "Buddy," I said, "you'd think being eight feet tall you'd have some room for brains." Then I reared back and hurled the egg at him. It exploded on his fore-head. There was a bright purple flash of light and a release of brimstone. Madgogg stopped dead, his face covered in a thick, black yolk. It oozed down his chin and fell in fat drops onto the floor.

Then—

Madgogg grabbed me by the throat with his big, meaty hands and lifted me. Oswald made some snide comment about a zom-bie omelet, but I was too busy trying to keep my head attached to my body to pay him any mind.

"But I just destroyed your soul!" I shouted, though it sounded more like a whisper from a frog with laryngitis.

"Not my soul," the ogre grumbled.

Oswald said, "But I went to Black Rock and got the goose from the jackal, like you said in the cell."

"This jackal," the ogre said, "did he have a bushy tail and a white-gray coat?"

"Yeah."

"Your jackal was a coyote. I think his name is Sam."

I sunk my teeth into the ogre's arm—and nearly broke them. I had never tried to eat an ogre before, and I didn't think I would be trying that again. Their skin is tougher than petrified troll.

I heard a sickly tear from the back of my neck. It was just a matter of time before I was beheaded.

"Reginald Belial Madgogg, take your hands off that disgusting corpse!" a voice squealed.

Instantly the ogre dropped me and I crashed to the floor. When I looked up, I saw Willa standing in the doorway. The ogre rushed over to her. She wagged a finger at him and he shuffled his feet.

I stood up.

"Willa, you're free!" I said, too stupid to realize what was going on.

"Of course I'm free. Why shouldn't I be?"

"Let's get out of here."

"Why would I do that? We're getting married. Right, Reginald?"

The ogre nodded, stared at the floor.

I saw my fairy dust blowing into the four winds, an imminent zombie rampage in downtown ShadowShade. "But, Willa," I said, "your mother hired me to—"

"Listen, you stupid carcass, getting married was *my* idea—no matter what my bigoted mother might think. In fact, it took a bit of chasing and prodding to get this dumb oaf to finally propose. You and my mother won't stop that!"

"But he locked you in the dungeon."

"It wasn't locked, you brain-licking ghoul. We're in the middle of converting the dungeon into my boudoir. It's the only room in the house that doesn't stink like hellhound soup."

"Well *something* sure stinks around here."

"And what's this talk about destroying souls?"

I remained silent, and then Madgogg said, "Remember, honey, what I told you before about giving you my soul as a wedding gift? Well, I actually had it shipped here this morning. It was going to be a surprise. But considering what just happened..."

The ogre retrieved the small wooden box from the front table.

It was nearly identical to the one I retrieved from the goose's insides.

"My soul, my love," he said and handed her the box.

This ogre really was a smooth-talker.

"Thanks for ruining the surprise, *corpse!*" Willa spat. "Reginald wants to stick your head on his trophy wall, but the idea of looking at your rotten, dead face every day gives me the willies. So get out of here before I change my mind. And tell my mother the wedding is happening whether she likes it or not."

"Well, it looks like our business here is done," I said. "Good luck to the both of you. You'll need it." To Oswald, I said, "You're completely useless, you know that? If I don't get that fairy dust, I'm eating you first."

EPILOGUE

"It was a lovely wedding, wasn't it, Jack?" Oswald said.

I took a deep drag of my hellfire stick and then threw back a shot of Devil Boy.

"Would have been nice if they had a bottle of formaldehyde. No one considers zombies."

Madgogg insisted we come to the ceremony as his guests. Probably to piss off his new mother-in-law. I didn't need much prodding to piss off Gwendolyn. That was the last time I'd take a job from those double-crossing pixies.

"I did find the goose pâté in bad taste," Oswald said.

"I got my fairy dust. That's all I care about."

"But there's one thing that's still bothering me."

"Oswald, you're such a woman."

"Whose soul did you destroy?"

"Listen, souls are destroyed every day. Such is the cruel world of Pandemonium. Besides, what are the odds of it ever getting back to us?" I looked out my office window and watched a black-winged nightmare glide east toward the Broken Lands, a limp elf in its talons.

Oswald shrugged. I poured myself another hit of Devil Boy, but the intercom buzzed before I could throw it back.

"Yeah, Lilith?"

"There's a rather large and angry ogress here."

I looked at Oswald. He started morphing into a blob. That was a bad sign.

"Yeah, Lilith, what does she want?"

"Something about her recently deceased husband and a coyote named Sam."

I wondered if the fire escape would hold my weight. It had been a while since I last used it.

"Thanks, Lilith. Oswald will be right out."

BONUS MATERIAL

INCIDENT
ON BLACK ROCK

This is the account Oswald filed after his mission to Black Rock. I don't believe a word of it. – Jack

MISSION: DJ-7845
LOCATION: BLACK ROCK, UNDEAD SEA
AGENT: OSWALD

The RavenHawk copter cut through the Pandemonium sky like dragon's fire through a dwarf village. The violent waters of the Undead Sea churned below, black waves thundering up toward the underside of the flying craft. I squinted toward the horizon and spied a dark speck.

Moments later, the pilot's voice crackled over the com line: "We have visual confirmation of Black Rock. Are you in position, Agent Oswald?"

I stood in the open doorway of the aerial machine. "Affirmative," I spit into the helmet mic.

I watched as the dark speck grew like a giant rising from his slumber. This was Black Rock! The humungous chunk of obsidian sat motionless, magically floating forty yards above the water, which somehow remained calm and unmoving.

I sat on the edge of the doorway. Now I could see that the rock's surface was irregularly shaped, filled with deep craters and crevices, overhangs and projections.

The RavenHawk hovered one klick from the eastern edge of Black Rock.

"Prepare for descent," the pilot said.

The chopper descended. I tossed off my helmet and dove into the Undead Sea.

I watched as the RavenHawk shot away from Black Rock. I had ordered the pilot to stay at least five klicks from its shore so as not to alert the infernal beasts. I had one hour to complete my mission and rendezvous with the copter. If I didn't make it back in time, the RavenHawk was ordered to leave without me. Failure was not an option.

I swam through the maniac waves until I came to the calm waters surrounding Black Rock. When I reached the edge of the suspended stone, I stretched my right arm to its breaking part. I barely gained purchase on a tiny protrusion, but it was all I needed to pull myself up.

I crawled and climbed and struggled to the surface. I stood on Black Rock and was greeted by a sign. It read: MEHMET'S SOUL SECURITY AND PETTING ZOO.

I was in the correct place. Mehmet must be the demon in charge.

Finding the jackal shouldn't be too difficult, I thought. The real problem would be the five demons who guard the place. But I had a plan. A well-thought-out plan.

1) Morph into a worm, to disguise myself from the demonic horde.

2) Find the jackal by systematically searching the area.

3) Use a feather coated in peanut butter to make the jackal puke up the goose.

4) Use the same feather on the goose to make him puke up the box containing the ogre's soul.

5) Get off the damn rock.

As I wormed my way down a steep grade, I noticed the quiet—even the sounds of the Undead Sea had been silenced here. Then I noticed the stench. It was a mixture of brimstone, animal waste, and impending doom. I knew I was close.

The grade flattened for a short jog and then, over a short rise, I spotted the soul keepers.

The animals didn't make a noise. Pigs, ponies, goats, donkeys, and zebras languidly roamed as if sedated inside a clearing encircled by high stone walls. I didn't see the jackal.

I slid under a gate and entered the animal pen.

The stench had grown tenfold. But that was the least of my problems. A worm isn't the safest animal inside a zoo. Pigs clomped beside me and ponies peed on my back. If it wouldn't have drawn attention to me, I would have morphed into a lion. My limited field of vision increased the difficulty in locating the jackal, as all I could see were hooves. Stick to the plan, I told myself.

After mentally dividing the pen into quadrants, I began my systematic search.

The discovery of a tawny paw nearly had me jumping for joy, but it turned out to be a hyena's.

A raven landed several feet before me and pecked at the ground. The bird seemed more animated and lively than the others. Perhaps he wasn't one of them but had flown into the pen from the outside. Either way, I didn't like it.

The raven moved toward another fissure in the ground and probed it with his sharp beak. He seemed to be searching for something. Most likely food. The raven's pecking rang out in the silence. When I remembered that I was a worm, I headed in the opposite direction as quickly as possible. The pecking stopped suddenly and I could feel the raven's beady eyes on my back. I hastened my squirming, but a pig hoof clomped directly in my path. Black wings cracked like bullwhips. I tried to slink around the pig knuckles, but the raven was on me. The winged nightmare snatched me up and threw me into his yawning mouth. He swallowed me whole.

I was correct about the raven not being a member of Mehmet's Soul Security and Petting Zoo. There was no other animal or soul box inside his insides. Just little ol' me. In the darkness, I felt the bird rise. The mission had been compromised! The raven could be heading for Witch End for all I knew! I had to act fast.

I asked the bird for forgiveness and then I inflated my body, expanding like a balloon attached to a firehose.

The bird had indeed been in flight. Fortunately he hadn't gotten very far. Unfortunately he exploded directly above the five demons of Black Rock.

I crash-landed on top of a round stone table, around which sat the dark figures. They resembled shadows. If shadows wore black robes and had eyes like the tips of red-hot pokers.

"What in the name of Lucifer is that?" a demon cried as he extended a long, bony finger toward me. The other infernal creatures held playing cards. I sat on top of a heap of gold coins.

Another demon rose and shouted, "Don't use a distraction. You cheated me, Mehmet!"

"Sit down, Azazel, and deal!"

"But what of this?" Mehmet said and pointed at me with more emphasis.

"What?" a third demon asked. "Near that slug?"

"No, fool. The slug itself!"

"I believe it is a worm," Mehmet said.

"It's much too fat to be a worm. And where are its segments?"

Damn! I had forgotten segments! I instantly formed them, but only slightly, so as not to alert the demons to my mistake.

Mehmet looked closer at me and said, "I see the segments, fool! It is a worm!"

"A pretty poor worm, if you ask me."

I didn't let the slight bother me. I remained calm as Mehmet picked me up and held me in his palm, which he then held out. All five demons now stood and ogled me with infernal curiosity. I squirmed to the left and right to give the creatures a better look.

Mehmet giggled.

This seemed to bewilder the other demons.

"What was that queer sound you uttered?" Azazel asked as he leaned forward and studied me more intently.

Mehmet looked confused as well. After a long silence, he said, "I was merely clearing my throat."

I squirmed some more and the demon's giggle turned into a laugh.

His nefarious cohorts gasped.

"Your face has changed!" one of the demons said. "What has happened to your grimace?"

"What is this nonsense?" Mehmet said.

I really laid it on, doing a boogie-woogie in the demon's palm, my body rubbing against his black palm.

The dark lord jiggled and wiggled and laughed.

"He is making merry!" shouted Azazel.

"I never knew it possible," another demon said.

"I should like to make merry, too," yet another creature said. "Hand over that worm!"

But Mehmet's merriment had overwhelmed him and he ignored their pleas to enjoy me as well.

"Hold out your palm!" a demon said to Azazel. He did and the demon tickled his fiendish friend. Azazel tittered. The demon tickled more furiously and Azazel's titter turned into a guffaw.

"Do me!" the others shouted, and soon all the demons were tickling each other and laughing like schoolchildren. Eventually they all ended up on the ground, rolling in hysterics.

I made my escape.

Fortunately the demons' poker table was perched above the animal pen. From my higher vantage point, I was able to spot the jackal. (He really did look like a jackal.) The canine walked in a circle in the northwestern quadrant.

I morphed back to my old self and jumped into the pen.

I removed a sack that I had ensconced in my innards. Inside the sack was the peanut-butter-covered feather. I cornered the animal against the rock wall and waved the feather in front of his snout. He ignored it and stared up at me.

I thought for sure he wouldn't be able to resist peanut butter!

I tried to shove the feather in its mouth, but the animal refused to unclench its teeth.

By my calculations, I had only another fifteen minutes before the RavenHawk returned.

I knew of only one other way to induce vomiting: vomit yourself.

Without a digestive system, I needed to fake it. I turned to the side and began to heave and gag. The canine looked at me curiously. His stomach seemed to tighten. Was it working? I retched harder. The jackal/coyote seemed to choke, but he did not puke.

I fell to the ground writhing in fake pain, gagging like a sick kraken. He stuck his snout in my face and began to lick me. I didn't hesitate. I shoved the feather down his throat. I jumped up and pushed the feather deep into his innards.

The canine heaved. A large lump appeared in his neck and then with a large burp his jaws parted. Vomit geysered out and hit me directly in the face. A small, white goose followed, smacking into my midsection and landing on the ground awkwardly.

Dazed, it hopped up on its feet and blinked.

I held the feather at the ready, but then I noticed the demons' laughter had subsided. Now there was less than ten minutes to rendezvous with the RavenHawk. I grabbed the goose and shoved him inside my sack.

I raced to the edge of Black Rock and dove into the Undead Sea. Mission accomplished! (Sort of. Could you tell the difference between a coyote and a jackal, you dead dummy?)

ACKNOWLEDGMENTS

First and foremost, my thanks to Louis Schroeder, who employed his ninja skills to help make this book a reality. Ed Watson's incredible artwork turned this little project into a big project. I can't thank him enough for the huge amount of effort he put into this. Eve Conte Seligman edited this book not once, but twice, and saved me quite a lot of embarrassment. My thanks to her as well as Dave Seligman, who contributed his InDesign expertise and answered all of my annoying questions. My thanks to Tim Marquitz, who helped me to bring emotion to the story. John Harlacher has done so much to bring this project to life and to a wider audience that I'll always be in his debt.

There were many folks who helped out with the Kickstarter campaign, offering their work or advice. My thanks in particular to DeAnna Knippling, Doug Draa, John Betancourt, Steven Gladin, Alex Shvartsman, and Margot Atwell.

My wife, Jennifer, has always been my first reader and biggest supporter. Thank you, sweetie!

And of course a big thank-you to all the Kickstarter backers. Without them, this book wouldn't have been half as cool. Turn the page for a list of all these awesome people.

DEAD JACK
KICKSTARTER BACKERS

- Mary D'Ambrosio
- Sara and Louis Schroeder
- Angela Schroeder
- Nancy, Nick, and Ryan Nicotera
- Roger Beckett
- DeAnna Knippling
- Eric Allen
- Beth Cato
- Juliana Rew
- John Rap (Creator of Electromagnate)
- David Quist
- David O'Hanlon
- Kyle Erha
- Christopher "Ju Ju" Merrill
- Mel Torrella
- J.W. Craft II
- Emily Sunnucks
- Michelle Muhs
- Philip Gunsaules
- A.J. Reta
- Jackson Coates
- Garry Kraft
- Rob Steinberger
- Mike Evans
- Eric "Tuckmeister" Tucker
- Trent "Goregasm23" Tomlinson
- Jorge Urdiain
- Stacey L. Hallock
- Mike "Shack" Shackelford
- Nikolai Go Tenazas
- Thomas Saboy
- David Cason
- KMC
- Taz
- Monty Mantione
- John Ayers, Abdicated King of Sensible Castle of Ireland AKA Episkopos Dilligaf I; Hail Eris!
- Joe Stech
- Tyler Taute
- Darren A Atkinson
- Ariel Bermudo
- Nathaniel O'Coin
- Beardeadbully
- Archigan
- Zivan Denney
- Mark R. Lesniewski
- Xavier Lambercy
- Jay Spence
- Joe Pate
- Katrina Plonczynski
- Brook
- Flint & Steel
- Jeff C
- John M. Creagar
- Dave Ambrose
- Lark Cunningham
- Kris Mellinger
- Sam Norman
- Anders M. Ytterdahl
- Nicholas Crawford
- Nick Sharps
- veandr
- thatraja
- Mike Rider
- Marc Margelli
- John MacLeod
- Dave Luxton

- Oliver Weber
- Justin Noppé
- Kaos Kreegan
- João Pedro Lemos Petter
- Oliver Longchamps
- Pippa Bailey
- Caro Wick
- Jens Schumacher
- "The Magnificent" Joel Villis
- Faye Hartley
- Tom Hoefle
- Charles Fridge
- Josh Evans
- Jack Hickey
- Rory V. Block
- Ben Berger
- Martin Paytok
- Jim Giering
- Ethan Michel
- Joe Pulver's Mustache
- The Hand of Nyarlathotep
- Michael Fowler
- Melissa Bryan
- Lydia Miranda Medina
- Andrew N Ferguson
- Arran Dickson
- Erich Buchrieser
- Xavier Riesco
- Kathleen Fincham
- Ian Washburn
- Tyler Evans
- Kimberly Cowan
- Derek Abbott
- Fizaye
- Alexander Gudenau
- Nathaniel Trusting
- Ed Dexter
- Luke Spook
- Mandy Lawyer
- James Cleaveley
- Lady Rissa Moore
- Tony and Theresa Grey
- Beth McCloy
- David "subQuark" Miller
- Cole Kidd
- Jim & Paula Kirk
- Matthew Agle
- Stop Short
- Trevor Wayne Phillips
- Jay Brigman
- Kathy Maloy
- Will Q
- Jose Gonzalez
- Tim Migliore
- Eric Sowder
- Kai Fraass
- Garrett Calcaterra
- Randy P. Belanger
- Sandra Diaz
- Stephanie Wagner
- Christopher Michael Bones
- David Ross
- Roberto Carlos Carrillo Torres
- Thomas Ling
- Trystan Vel
- Bruce Deniston
- Kevin Purtell
- John Bowen
- Stefan M. Moser
- Teri Keas
- Stephen Duke Lord
- Michael Scholz
- Caitlin Jane Hughes
- James Thunberg
- eric priehs
- Jessie Gary
- Tony Muzi
- Peter Kelly
- Russell Roberto
- jamie cutler
- James P. Barbaro
- Formium Gotten

- Jillyjally
- Lizz Lektrik
- Sheldon Smith
- Sarah Gaulden
- Dean b lynch
- Dan A Nelson
- Callum E. Moore
- Richard Bartisek
- Jeff Weber
- Kenneth Lee Holliday, Jr.
- Keelee von Cupcake
- Laura Rushing
- Jason T Blackstone
- Jess White
- Zachariah M. Long
- William Groat
- Scott P Berger
- Victor C. Pelletier, Jr.
- Amanda Evans Mahony
- Steven Jasiczek
- Andrew M Poirier
- Pamela St Joseph
- Andy Beer
- Bryan Geddes
- Robert Lee Geddes
- Dimosthenis Mplatsis
- John Wharton
- JGoodwin
- Ghastly Games
- Ioannis Cleary
- Pedro Alfaro
- Dark Bisounours
- Brent Glenn
- JubJub Newman
- Victoria Griffiths
- Kieran Smith
- Matej Pupacic
- The Warped One
- SwordFire
- Constance Fletcher
- Joe Bertucci
- Clark Newton
- Robert Young
- Pontus Benom
- Kirstie Summers
- Brandon Salkil
- Amanda Raymond
- Stuart Hilsmier
- Luis A Pritchett
- Jeff Mires
- Jo B. Hayve
- Luke Steele
- Andrew and Kate Barton
- Chris Fritz
- Joyce Torme
- Matthew Avritt
- Sandy Thorn
- Mobtek
- Alexander Lepera
- Blake Standard
- Michael Valenzuela
- Krystin Eaton and Zane Winkelman
- Snicker Furfoot
- Kristoffer B Hansson
- Michael Burton
- Amanda Pack
- Ynara Camargo
- Ahmet N. Sati
- Piranhatron3000
- David Perlmutter
- Carrick Maile
- Richard Nettleton
- Ted Nichols
- Chris Moo Mutz
- Michael Assante
- Elethia Rex
- Tabitha Wilson
- Krikkit[ONE]

ABOUT THE AUTHOR

James Aquilone was raised on Saturday morning car-toons, comic books, sitcoms, and Cap'n Crunch. Amid the Cold War, he dreamed of being a jet fighter pilot but decided against the military life after realizing it would require him to wake up early. He had further illusions of being a stand-up comedian, until a traumatic experience on stage forced him to seek a college education. Brief stints as an alternative rock singer/ guitarist and child model also proved unsuccessful. Today he battles a severe chess addiction while trying to write in the speculative fiction game.

His short fiction has been published in such places as Nature's Futures, *The Best of Galaxy's Edge 2013-2014*, *Unidentified Funny Objects 4*, and Weird Tales magazine. Suffice it to say, things are going much better than his modeling career.

James lives in Staten Island, New York, with his wonderful wife, Jennifer.